Sergeant Jack

Also by John David Harris M.Ed.

Beyond the Cattle Arch

Straw Hat

The Truth About Melanie

For more of John's books, visit
www.jdhwriterandartist.com/library

Sergeant Jack

John David Harris M.Ed.

The manufacturer's authorised representative in the EU for product
safety is Authorised Rep Compliance Ltd, 71 Lower Baggot Street,
Dublin D02 P593 Ireland (www.arccompliance.com)

This is a work of fiction. Names, characters, businesses, places, events
and incidents are either the products of the author's imagination
or used in a fictitious manner. Any resemblance to actual persons,
living or dead, or actual events is purely coincidental.

Troubador Publishing Ltd
Unit E2 Airfield Business Park,
Harrison Road, Market Harborough,
Leicestershire LE16 7UL
Tel: 0116 279 2299
Email: books@troubador.co.uk
Web: www.troubador.co.uk

ISBN 978-1-83628-033-0

British Library Cataloguing in Publication Data.
A catalogue record for this book is available from the British Library.

Printed and bound by CPI Group (UK) Ltd, Croydon, CR0 4YY
Typeset in 11pt Georgia by Troubador Publishing Ltd, Leicester, UK

For my father, Jack Harris

Chapter 1

IF EVER THERE existed a misnomer, it must surely be Wellborn Street, situated as it was in the poverty-stricken area of Whitechapel. It was a borough of London and, in the 1870s, deprivation and food shortages hung over the area like a dark cloud.

Somehow, even during the summertime, the sun seemed hard-pressed to penetrate the local canyon-like roads where the tiny terraced houses sat gazing forlornly at each other across the narrow little streets – streets so narrow that neighbours could peg out lines of washing suspended from their first-floor windows. Although how they remained clean in the smog-laden atmosphere during winter was a mystery, for even the bricks were stained a dark grey from the constant belching of black smoke from the numerous and cramped chimney stacks.

Arguably, it was the children who suffered most; often hungry and ill-equipped – especially during the colder months – it was not uncommon to see young children playing barefoot in the street. This level of deprivation combined with unsanitary living conditions often resulted in a high infant mortality rate. This was late in the nineteenth century and some time before the sweeping changes ushered in by the First World War. It was an era, in fact, when the rich were very wealthy and the rest...

However, not everyone in Wellborn Street had always lived on the poverty line. Number 13 was the home of Brian Jackson and his wife, Ada, and in the early days of their married life, they had both enjoyed full employment.

In many ways, they were physically similar. Brian was by no means a tall man. However, he was very strong for his limited stature. His slightly younger wife was sturdily built and many men would have found her far from attractive. In fact, with her short cropped black hair and lack of any obvious feminine characteristics, "butch" would probably have been the word that sprang to mind. But Brian had found her attractive and, certainly in the early days, had loved her very dearly until...

Brian had left school when barely eleven and gone straight into the bakery business as an errand boy, but upon reaching the age of twenty, had been promoted to the lofty position of driving a one-horse delivery van. It was in this capacity that he had met his future wife, who had been the resident cook at one of the big houses south of the river. There had been no instant passion, but every few days, when he dropped off the regular bread order, they seemed to get a little closer.

Brian had found the relationship initially hard going – not so much through any fault of the lady, but rather his own inhibiting shyness. A shyness undoubtedly fostered by having been an only child, while the courting ground itself was far from conducive to romance, being, as it was, the lower ground-floor entrance to the servants' quarters. One day, however, events seemed to take an upward turn when Ada invited him in through to the main staff kitchen.

At least, it seemed a step forward before he actually saw the scale of activities that were going on there, for this was life downstairs where armies of underpaid skivvies sacrificed their lives in order to smooth the way of the few living above.

Compared to his parents' tiny scullery in Kipper Street, the area was enormous and dominated by a table capable of seating at least a dozen people. Not that anyone was actually sitting down because the upstairs fraternity were obviously in demanding mode. Housemaids scurried about everywhere as they flapped and flustered around various ironing boards and the stove. Their personalities seemed lost beneath a sea of black uniforms and white aprons, but the chief housemaid obviously knew them all.

'Eva, don't forget Lord Grant likes his cufflinks and collar studs in place when you take up those shirts. And hurry! You know what his wife can be like if she thinks it's getting late.'

And so, the buzz ebbed and flowed as if Brian was not even there. However, what none of them could have known was how this time-honoured and, in some ways, secure way of life was in its declining years, for the German kaiser's army was soon to put a stop to this centuries-old, privileged social structure.

In sharp contrast to all the hassle around him, one man sat quietly eating his breakfast – a man who Brian instantly recognised by his immaculate tailored suit as the head butler.

'Good morning, baker,' he greeted the new arrival, putting down his cup and reaching for a napkin. 'Still raining out there?' It was, of course, an almost irrelevant question, for in that part of London it never seemed to be anything other than "raining out there". The butler slowly wiped his mouth. 'You must be pretty exposed to the weather in that open-fronted van of yours.'

Brian dumped his heavy basket on the kitchen table with a certain relief.

'Well, strictly speakin',' he explained, 'it ain't my van. It belongs to the firm, but I'm okay with the oilskin and the 'orse 'as got a good weatherproof coat.'

'Do I detect a slight cockney accent?' said the listener, smiling as he got to his feet.

'Aye, yer do that!' exclaimed the delivery man in his brusque way. 'Kipper Street, born and bred. And proud of it. Number 9 to be exact and close to that wonderful St Mary-le-Bow. I go there every Sunday.' He paused as if embarrassed, then added, 'A man should do what he thinks is right.'

'Indeed,' said the butler, nodding. 'Indeed, he should.'

Brian had strung together more words at that

point than he would normally use in a day. A man of dour disposition, he had never made a point of socialising – neither had he any experience with the ladies. It had only been Ada's unfailing welcoming smile that had aroused his interest.

As Brian had rightly observed, the head butler was a man of smart appearance with his carefully oiled and combed-back hair and thin, manicured moustache. He commanded an air of respect. Nevertheless, beneath this professional exterior lurked a kind disposition.

'Look, Ada!' he exclaimed, having sensed a budding connection between her and the delivery man. 'Why don't you invite your friend to take the weight off his feet and offer him a cup of tea.'

'Thank you, Arthur.' She smiled as he left to attend to the numerous demands of the day.

'Ah! Nice man yer've got there,' commented Brian, taking a seat at the huge table.

'Yes, he's lovely,' agreed Ada, placing two cups on the table.

Silence reigned for a moment.

Now, her companion was not only slightly socially awkward, but also tended to blurt things out before first thinking them through – a factor evidenced by what came next.

'I 'ear,' he said, slowly, 'there be a 'ouse to rent in Wellborn Street.'

'Oh,' she replied, holding her cup with her elbows on the table. 'I thought you lived with your parents in Kipper Street.'

'Aye, I do that,' confirmed Brian. At this point, he began to struggle. He knew what he had in mind but found it almost impossible to express. 'Eh. Yer don't understand,' he persisted. 'It's only two shillin' a week and some landlords in that street are askin' up to three and six. There be a livin' room with a fireplace and a big enamel bath, so yer could 'ave a warm wash in comfort. Then there's a scullery out back and a privy behind that.' As a final persuader, he added, 'And there're two bedrooms upstairs.'

The butler had returned in time to catch the end of this outpouring and gave Ada a knowing look, so that, finally, the implications of what she'd heard sank in.

'Brian!' she exclaimed. 'Is this some weird way of asking me to marry you?'

But the poor recalcitrant baker was finally and completely lost for words. This was not the case for Arthur and he wasted no time.

'I think, Ada, that's very much what this young man's proposing – and may I be the first to congratulate you.'

Unlike Brian, Ada came from a large family; so large, in fact, that when she'd joined Lord Grant's household as a trainee cook at the tender age of ten, it was doubtful whether she was even missed. It was also a fact that there was little emphasis on schooling before the Education Act of 1880, so nobody thought twice about employing children. However, glad of the opportunity, Ada had worked hard to become a valued member of the kitchen staff.

Now approaching her late teens, she had become

painfully aware of her lack of feminine attributes. Standing a mere five feet two, she could detect no sign of the curves so obvious in her fellow female servants and it had left her feeling bitter. She had accepted the unlikelihood of marriage and the probability of a lifetime of in-house service, so she was overcome by this unexpected turn of events.

'Brian,' she cried, throwing her arms around his neck. 'Is that really what you're trying to say?'

The poor baker felt as though he'd pulled his finger out of a dam and got caught up in the backwash.

'Ah, well,' he managed, finally, 'we'd 'ave to 'ave somewhere to live and I thought...'

Whatever it was that he thought was as far as he got, as Ada kissed him long and hard on the lips. But then, in the midst of all the euphoria, she was struck by a chilling thought.

Chapter 2

'ARTHUR,' ADA BEGAN anxiously. 'I'm in full-time service here. If I get married, how will that affect my job?'

'I think,' replied the head butler, 'that is something you would need to discuss with the lady of the house. I'll make an appointment for you to see her later in the week.'

Monday 5th and Thursday 8th October 1874 would prove landmarks in Ada's life that she would never forget. The Monday, in particular, made an enormous impact as someone had asked for her hand in marriage. Thursday, on the other hand, was quite a different proposition and one she faced with genuine trepidation.

All her working life had been spent downstairs in the dimly lit kitchen and the first thing that struck her as she approached the drawing room was how much lighter it seemed in the upper part of the house.

Her nervousness showed and the head butler, who was with her, smiled encouragingly as he tapped the door of the interview room.

'Come,' came the brief and immediate response of a woman's voice.

The impact of the room left Ada almost breathless. Brilliantly illuminated by classical Georgian windows, the area seemed vast with its deep pile and highly patterned Persian carpet. Then, straight ahead, a massive ornately carved marble fireplace seemed to dominate the far end of the room. Standing in front of it was a tall, slim man immaculately clad in the style of the era and sporting sideburns that virtually reached his shoulders.

Ada had never met him before, but, from his bearing, assumed him to be Lord Grant – who seemed to have acquired the irritating habit of rising and falling on the balls of his feet. It was a nervous habit, no doubt, developed by years of living with a domineering wife.

Either side of the chimney breast, floor-to-ceiling shelves stood packed with neatly aligned leather-bound volumes and, to the left, a three-fold screen depicted exotic birds from the east. To the right was a wide and delicately carved mahogany desk, behind which was the lady of the house, who was about to take her seat in a high-backed leather swivel chair.

Beautiful and haughty was an apt description. Thick, greying gold hair piled high on her head emphasised a slim neck, which was embellished with multiple rows of genuine pearls, while her off-the-shoulder designer dress plunged to a parting of the ways that most men would have died for. She exuded, in fact, the whole feminine elegance and power that poor Ada so sadly lacked. Glamorous, rich, sophisticated – the list was endless.

Once seated, the lady reached for a slim gold case and selected a cigarette, before fitting it into a thin holder. Then, still without saying a word, she lit it and proceeded to emit a long stream of smoke up towards the ornate ceiling. Finally, she looked at the head butler.

'Was there something, Arthur?'

If Arthur had been intimidated by the woman's condescending manner, he gave no sign of it. He was, indeed, a professional of the era through and through.

'Yes, my lady, there is. I don't think,' he added, indicating his companion, 'that you've met Ada. She's one of our very competent cooks and now has the opportunity of getting married.'

The expression on Lady Grant's face would have been difficult to describe.

'Really!'

'Basically, my lady,' he continued, 'we were wondering if she could retain her position here on a daytime basis.'

The imperious woman again drew on her cigarette.

'By "we",' she began acidly, 'I suppose you mean "she" was wondering if we could keep her on.' She sighed and raised her eyebrows in mock irritation. 'I see no reason why not – provided, of course, it in no way intrudes on the smooth running of our domestic arrangements. What do you think, Paul?' she added, turning to the man by the fireplace.

'Oh, yes, dear. That's fine. Anything that's okay with you is fine by me.'

Lord Grant was obviously a yes-man of the first order.

*

Early the following year, plain Miss Ada Brown became the proud Mrs Ada Jackson and the bells of the soaring St Mary-le-Bow pealed out their joyful celebration. It was Saturday 17th April 1875 and a beautiful spring afternoon, as the happy couple emerged from the ceremony as man and wife.

Churchyards are often a grim echo of life's finality with their leaning crosses and collapsing mausoleums, but on the occasion of the wedding all these reminders of ends were swallowed up by the promise of a new beginning. Primroses and daffodils abounded on every side. The daffodils, in particular, reflected the sun's brilliance and swayed in the gentle breeze, determined to welcome the couple to their new life. Everywhere, in fact, spring filled the air with the prospect of good times to come.

Each side of the path, bluebells struggled to make their way through a sea of buttercups and, as Ada stood by her new husband in the bright sunlight, she felt it would always be the happiest day of her life. In fact, she would sometimes refer to it as her "walk with the flowers". Unfortunately, the years ahead would prove to be anything but a floral dance.

Chapter 3

EARLY TIMES AT 13 Wellborn Street were relatively happy for Brian and Ada. Knowing he was not a particularly attractive man, he had been more than receptive to the attentions of the young cook. But sex is an independent force and not necessarily subservient to the mindset of the one it inhabits. From an evolutionist's perspective, it's an almost immortal power that has been honed over the millennia to seek out and reproduce the best of its particular kind. And, sadly, that drive within Brian slowly began to make him aware that Ada was very far from the best of her kind.

It was nothing sudden. He still loved his wife and enjoyed the fascination of life with the opposite sex. However, gradually, and over time, more curvaceous women came increasingly to his attention and made him wonder if he was missing out.

Initially, this had little apparent impact on their marriage and, after the first year, Ada fell pregnant. It was a financial blow for it spelt the end of her days as an in-house cook. However, this was partly offset by Brian's promotion to chief supervisor at the bakery firm. And, with careful planning, they just about managed. Then, on the stroke of midnight, Sunday 21st January 1877, their first son put in an appearance accompanied by an almighty yell. He was a boy who, as a man, was destined to study engineering and emigrate to America as the West was opening up and make a fortune in railway construction – but that's another story.

Even though they had a second son some eighteen months later, it did little to ease Brian's growing sense of sexual dissatisfaction. Not that he attempted to dally with other women – he didn't – but it badly affected his relationship with Ada as he felt less and less physically drawn to her.

At first, his wife tried to pretend he was just tired after the long hours demanded by his new position of authority, but, in the end, it was a pretence that became unsustainable and she had to admit something was seriously wrong. With his now being away for such long periods, the spectre of another woman arose in her mind. However, knowing Brian as she did, she felt it was an unlikely scenario. There had to be something else – but what?

Ada was approaching her mid-twenties, with all its accompanying physical needs. Brian always came to bed after her and automatically fell into a dead sleep – seemingly indifferent to whether she was awake or not. But on the night of 10th September 1878, she was determined to have it out with him once and for all and, grabbing his shoulder, shook him awake.

'What is it...? What's the matter?' he managed, a touch irritably.

'I'll tell you what's the matter, Brian!' she exclaimed in her rather butch way. 'You haven't approached me for sex in over six months and I want to know why.'

Chapter 4

PALE GASLIGHT FILTERED in through thin curtains from the street outside as Brian swung his legs over the side of the bed. Then, lifting the glass funnel of their oil lamp, he struck a match and applied it to the wick. The moment he feared had arrived and, in the new brighter light, he turned to face his disgruntled wife.

'We've been married for some three years now,' he began gently, 'and 'ave I ever given yer any cause to doubt me word?'

'Nooo...' she replied, resting back on her elbows, 'but...'

'The point is,' continued her husband, 'that although I love you very dearly and wouldn't swap you for anyone, my sex drive 'as never been the best. Well, certainly not if what I 'ear about some men is to be believed.' He hung his head. 'I'm sorry I can't be more for you.'

'Huh,' she retorted. 'There was nothing wrong with you the night we got married. What's happened? Got bored with me, have you?'

'It's nothing like that,' he replied reassuringly,

putting an arm round her shoulders. 'We're 'appy enough, aren't we? We've two lovely little boys and I promise to try 'arder.'

But Ada was not to be so easily placated and, with the hard side of her nature in full swing, she snapped, 'Oh, don't bother yourself if it takes all that effort.' And with that, she tore away from his embrace, before flouncing out of the room.

*

By the end of the following century, or even earlier, such a situation would almost certainly have ended in divorce. However, in the late 1800s, a woman had few options but to remain in a less-than-happy marriage. Meanwhile, as limited as Brian was in some respects, he persevered with their relationship and, little by little, the two slowly grew closer, but although he tried to be demonstrative, actual sex remained a rare occurrence.

Even so, and as a complete surprise, Ada gave birth to a third son some fourteen years later. It was Friday 7th October 1892 and the late nine o'clock chimes of St Mary-le-Bow had scarcely faded before the ensuing silence of 13 Wellborn Street was shattered by the new baby's cry. Ada and Brian now had a third son who, having come into the world so close to the famous church, was, like his siblings, technically a Cockney – a fact of which he was always proud, although, in reality, it was actually a derogatory term.

After his birth, Ada informed her husband that the new addition to their family should be known as Jack. 'Nothing else, mind you,' she insisted. 'Just Jack.'

Although the youngster already had two older brothers, they never really seemed to accept him and, to all intents and purposes, he might as well have been an only child in his early years. Furthermore, it was a small house for five and as Jack grew older, his two brothers, Walter and George, made it abundantly clear they had no desire to share their bedroom with a third person.

However, other factors were also beginning to worry Ada – not least of which was how tall and well-built Jack was becoming for his age, while her first two were very average. And by the time their third son reached eight, Brian commented on the fact.

He closed the door between the living room and scullery so no one else could hear.

'It's strange,' he mused idly, while helping to wash up in the cramped little room. 'Our Jack don't look much like either of us.' Then, hanging up the cups he'd just wiped, he added, 'Yer know, he's gonna be a big fella, so I'll 'ave to watch me ps and qs.'

Brian had said it in jest, but it struck a chord of horror in the heart of his wife and, later that week, her husband was to find out why.

*

The baker had never been either a socialiser or a man who cared much for drink – with the latter being further restricted by home commitments and a lack of money. The only exception to this austerity was a pint of lager once a week. The pub he frequented was situated on the corner of Wellborn Street and was known as The Broken Barrel. It had always been dimly lit by flickering oil lamps until recently and the fumes combined with the tobacco smoke had reduced the décor to a sticky yellow ochre. Nevertheless, the place always provided a welcome, if poky, atmosphere.

However, the atmosphere on the occasion in question was about to be torn apart by a sudden and explosive outburst of violence.

'Good evening, Brian,' greeted the one and only barmaid upon his arrival. 'Your usual pint?' she added, while reaching up for one of the tankards stored above the counter. The sensual action seemed to amplify her perhaps over-generous endowments and it immediately caught the attention of one of the male patrons.

Brian had been vaguely aware of a young man standing to his right. At well over six feet, the individual leaned across and muttered under his breath, 'I could well do that a power of good.'

It was crude and, initially, Ada's husband ignored him. It suddenly became painfully obvious that the speaker had no idea who Brian was when he added, 'Like I did with that bit at number 13 several years back.'

At this, everything suddenly flashed into focus in Brian's mind as he realised he was probably looking at Jack's real father. His reaction was immediate and instinctive. Although a good three or four inches shorter than the offender, he instantaneously sank his right fist deep into the man's windpipe with every ounce of strength he possessed. Brian was not a big man, but had a certain sinewy power. The result was devastating and the victim dropped slowly to the floor, gagging for breath.

The effect of this unexpected brutality in the little pub was electrifying, for, although situated in an essentially working-class area, it had always offered a sense of peace and relaxation.

White-faced, the barmaid gasped and said, 'Brian! What on earth...?'

But Brian was beyond control. The sanctity of his marriage had been violated. His wife had deceived him and, to a man of simple basic proprieties, the impact was unimaginable. Moreover, this was late Victorian England where the Ten Commandments still held a certain sway, unlike the melting pot of moral values to be witnessed by the twentieth-century Western world.

The barmaid had been in the process of filling Brian's tankard, but, lost in the red mists of absolute fury, he grabbed the vessel from her hand and smashed it down on the adulterer's head as he lay on the floor. Already blue in the face through lack of oxygen and with blood gushing from a deep wound in his forehead, he sank back and lay completely still.

The shrieking silence that followed was almost unimaginable, but as the barmaid rushed to assist the injured victim, it was broken by a man sitting next to the entrance.

'I don't suppose,' he began, in a surprisingly calm voice, 'that you know who that man is?'

Still almost insane with anger, Brian snarled, 'Do you think I care a fuck? That bastard committed adultery with my wife.' He started moving towards the door.

'You will!' exclaimed the speaker. 'Because that's James Van der Berg – the youngest son of London's chief magistrate.' However, he then made the fatal mistake of stepping into Brian's way and holding up a restraining hand. 'You're not going anywhere until the police arrive.' After witnessing events at the bar, the man was either very brave or downright stupid, because Brian still had the handle of the broken tankard in his hand – complete with its razor-sharp edges.

'Are you going to stop me, bastard?' he almost screamed while wielding the deadly shard.

But the "bastard", wary of the possible consequences, wisely moved aside.

Once outside the pub, Brian discarded the vicious piece of glass into the gutter as he strode along the narrow pavement to his home at number 13. It would be difficult, if not impossible, to describe his state of mind, for all normal perception of life had now gone out of focus while the structure and purpose of his world lay in ruins – a fact reflected, perhaps, by the ominous and threatening clouds that had now obscured an earlier bright moon. Finally, outside number 13, he buried his face in his hands in abject despondency, knowing that everything he held dear was about to come to an end.

Chapter 5

AFTER FLINGING THE front door open, he found his family sitting in their small living room. His wife and their three sons – only now, of course, it wasn't three sons, it was two. Ada was busily entertaining them with a game of snakes and ladders, and she looked up in surprise.

'Why, Brian!' she exclaimed, pleased to see him. 'I didn't expect you back so soon.'

The oil lamps in the background flickered intermittently and cast eerie shadows on the walls – almost, as it were, as if they sensed the disaster that was about to unfold. Indeed, seeing the expression on her husband's face, Ada instantly realised something was terribly wrong.

'Brian, what is it?' she asked, fearfully, getting to her feet.

He crashed his fist on the table with such force that it sent the board game and counters flying. The two older offspring had never seen anything like it and they cowed back in terror, while Jack clung tearfully to his mother.

'Who the bloody 'ell is James Van der Berg?' he almost screamed. 'Tell me. Who the 'ell is he?'

His wife's face became ashen as she turned to the children.

'Boys, go to your room until tomorrow.'

But Brian was beside himself.

'No, no. Let 'em know all about your disgusting behaviour. That boy's a bastard,' he shouted, pointing at Jack. 'A result of your adultery with this Van der Berg. And where did it all 'appen, huh?' he stormed. 'While I was away long hours working to maintain the home. In our bed, was it? Tell me. Was it in our own bed? Well, it'll be the last time he'll be so keen to violate someone else's marriage, because I've smashed a glass tankard over the bastard's head. So, if he lives, his face will be scarred for life.'

'Brian, please, please,' she begged. 'Not in front of the children.' And again, she ordered the youngsters to their rooms. Then, when the boys were finally gone, she turned to her husband. 'Brian, I assure you it only happened the once. I have told you time and time again that I've felt neglected. Months would pass with no physical contact at all and I have needs, Brian. I have needs.'

But he was beyond reason as he leaned his hands on the table.

'Once? Only once? Oh, that's alright then,' he shouted sarcastically. 'I tell you what. There's no way I'm working to provide a roof for that little bastard upstairs.' Turning to leave, he added, 'When I get back, make sure he's gone and don't you dare ever let me catch you call 'im by my name. Call 'im what you bloody well like, but not Jackson.'

And, with that, he stormed out and slammed the door, leaving his wife in floods of tears and with no idea of what to do next. But if the frightful scene had affected Ada, it had a far greater and lasting impact on the trembling little Jack up in their bedroom, for, being a small house, he had heard every word. Moreover, and poignantly, when Brian closed the front door so violently, it was to prove the last time that Jack would ever see the man he thought to be his father.

Ada's terror of Brian's reaction if he returned to find Jack still at home proved unfounded, because as her husband tramped the streets that night with a mind in turmoil, he was arrested. Van der Berg miraculously survived the brutal attack, but his father was determined to exact suitable retribution – a determination that was to see a twenty-year sentence handed down to Brian for his criminal assault.

In turn, this had a devastating financial effect on 13 Wellborn Street, for, with no income from the bakery, the situation immediately became untenable. Fortunately, Ada had a number of brothers and sisters who were prepared to take in the children, while, almost unbelievably, Lord and Lady Grant were gracious enough to allow her to resume in-house service at their mansion. Sadly, therefore, the little house in Wellborn Street ceased to exist as a home.

Even sadder, perhaps, was Jack's parting with his mother. Largely rejected by his two older brothers, he had become almost solely dependent on her and now, for reasons not clear in his young mind, she was going to desert him.

'When will I see you and Daddy again?' he cried pathetically.

In her heart, Ada felt torn apart knowing that this tragedy had been brought about by her own wrongdoing. She was also bitterly aware that, once back in service, there would be scant chance of ever seeing her little son again.

*

The sister who had agreed to take responsibility for Jack was an entirely different proposition to his mother – which was largely due to the grandmother's second marriage. Younger than Ada, she was a tall, elegant blonde. Moreover, she lived in a highly residential area on the outskirts of Croydon – a wide avenue that afforded beautifully appointed and double-fronted detached bungalows. A world away, in fact, from the dinge that had been Wellborn Street.

Sitting there in her sister's light and spacious reception room, Ada let her eyes wander over its obvious extravagance. Hand-painted Doulton vases adorned the marble mantlepiece, while opposite stood a glass-fronted mahogany showcase filled with delicate porcelain figurines. Then, deep-pile white carpet covered the entire floor and gracing the bay window was an ornately carved table topped by a cut-glass vase that contained a riot of flowers – blossoms that not only reflected colour and light, but seemed to gaze longingly at their free counterparts beyond the mullion window.

Looking across at her sister sitting opposite, Ada observed enviously, 'You really do have a beautiful home here, Eva, and I'm so grateful to you for taking in my little Jack.'

The younger woman tucked up her shapely legs onto her armchair.

'Yes,' she admitted, 'it's pleasant enough – although the neighbours are not much to go by.'

'Why?' began Ada. 'It's a nice enough area...'

Eva shrugged. 'Oh, they just don't seem very friendly.'

What Ada couldn't know was that the neighbours had good reason not to be friendly, for beneath Eva's apparent opulence, there lurked a dark secret. Though there was no proof, it was rumoured that she was, in fact, a high-society prostitute. Needless to say, Ada had no inkling of this when she bade her little boy goodbye – a goodbye symbolic of the fact that, in all probability, she would never see him again.

*

Jack's aunt proved a kind woman and, over the ensuing years, he grew quite fond of her – although one thing in the early days caused him a great deal of anxiety. There were occasions when she would be out all night, having left strict instructions not to answer the door to anyone. It was only much later, after a violent episode, that the reasons for these absences became apparent.

However, in the meantime, Eva's priority was to enrol her new protégé at one of the recently established junior schools. It was here that the young boy experienced another blow destined to affect his attitude in later life. Seeing a new boy in her class, the teacher asked his name.

'Jack,' replied Ada's son, hesitantly.

She nodded before enquiring his surname.

Too terrified to use the name Jackson, he stuttered, 'I... I... It's just Jack, Miss. I ain't got no other name.'

And that was the start of his misery as he heard a girl behind him giggle and parrot to her neighbour, 'Jack Sprat could eat no fat. His wife could eat no lean.'

In some perverse way, children can enjoy being cruel. It caught on and, after that, everywhere the new boy went, he was followed by an endless chanting of 'Jack Sprat, Jack Sprat.' Often when he turned around, there would be no one there and his life gradually became a misery – to the point where he began to dread going to school.

One day, he stepped into the playground and the teasing began immediately. Now, Jack was big for his age and, in a burst of sudden fury, he grabbed the nearest offender and flung him to the ground, but, upon seeing this, the tormentor's cohorts piled into Jack and brought him down. Against such odds, Ada's son had no chance and the duty teacher was momentarily out of sight.

However, help was at hand in the form of an older pupil, who dived to Jack's rescue. Handy with his fists, Jack's ally didn't hold back and several bloodied noses were the result.

Once it was over, Ada's son held out his hand. 'Thanks. I get so fed up with being teased.'

His new friend nodded. 'Yes, I'd heard some of it,' he replied. 'By the way, my name's Michael. Michael Miles.'

It was to be the start of a close and enduring friendship, which would last up to and almost throughout the First World War.

*

By the time Jack reached twelve, it was 1904 and he'd left school to become an apprentice butcher at Brownlow & Son in the centre of Croydon. However, the hands of time were ticking down to the First World War. In the meantime, Ada's son proved himself a worthy employee and, one morning, his boss called him over to the chopping board where he had been busy carving chops.

'You know, Jack,' he began, wiping the blood on his striped apron. 'You've been one of the best assistants I've had.' Turning to sharpen his knife on the butcher's steel, he asked, 'How old are you now?

About eighteen?' When Jack nodded, the butcher added, 'I don't want to stand in your way, but there's a vacancy come up at the Croydon abattoir. The money's good and you're a big strong lad. Mind you,' he cautioned, 'you've got to have the stomach for that kind of work.'

As Jack went to reply, a lady entered the shop.

'Good morning, Mr Brownlow. Good morning, Jack,' she said, with a slightly flirtatious flutter of her eyelashes.

Jack, however, didn't want to know and just nodded, before leaving his boss to attend to the customer's needs. He'd spent six happy years at the butcher, got on well with his employer and generally enjoyed the social interaction with the customers – all of which made him wary of change, no matter the financial reward.

However, if Jack had learnt one lesson in life, it was that everything does change, whether it be slowly or suddenly – like the loss of his family life in Wellborn Street. He gazed round at his familiar workplace: the worn and grooved chopping block that formed the main counter; the sawdust-covered floor that soaked up the steady drip of blood from a row of beef carcasses on the opposite wall. He switched his attention to the busy thoroughfare beyond the shop window – all so much part of his world. *Do I really want to change all that?* he asked himself.

*

Later that evening, as Jack turned into his aunt's avenue, his mind was still wrestling with the dilemma over his job. As he got closer to her bungalow, he was surprised to notice a gleaming open-topped car parked outside. In 1910, cars of any sort were a rare sight and this was a particularly magnificent model. With its shiny red paintwork and polished brass headlamps, Jack immediately recognised it as a two-seater Daimler Coupe, which, together with its uniformed chauffeur, spoke of only one thing. Money! However, Jack couldn't imagine what it was doing outside his aunt's house – although he was about to find out.

Placing his key in the front door lock, he was horrified to hear his aunt's repeated screams and, bursting into the lounge, could hardly believe his eyes. An obviously very prosperous man, who had allowed his prosperity to accumulate largely round his midriff, was brutally holding his aunt with one hand while slapping her about with the other.

Now, as his boss had pointed out, Jack was a big lad for his age and he wasted no time. His aunt had been good to him and lovingly nursed him through the loss of his home and his mother.

Furiously, he grabbed the fat man away from his aunt and sank his right fist deep into the offender's stomach. Air whooshed from the man's lungs as he doubled over as far as his bloated midriff would allow. Not content, Eva's infuriated nephew drove the same fist into the intruder's face, whereupon the offender collapsed across the brass fender with a resounding crash and lay half in and half out of the fireplace.

In the meantime, Jack turned to his sobbing aunt and took her into his arms.

'What on earth is that man doing here?' he asked.

She looked up at him with red-rimmed tear-stained eyes.

'Oh, Jack,' she murmured. 'It's a long story.' Unable to meet his gaze, she looked away. 'You see,' she began, in a broken voice, 'there were thirteen of us children originally – all crammed into a small apartment in Kipper Street. And we were poor, Jack,' she sobbed. 'Miserably and grindingly poor. Night after night, we would go to bed hungry.' As she spoke, the gross visitor began struggling to his feet amid a clattering of the fire irons.

'Excuse me a moment,' said Jack. 'I want a word in this creature's ear.' Lifting the man up by the lapels, he hissed, 'If ever I see you within a mile of this bungalow, there won't be enough left of you to scrape into a matchbox. Now, have you got that?'

'I've got it,' muttered the victim through bruised and swollen lips.

'Now, get the hell out of here while you still can,' snarled Jack.

And with that, the obese abuser made his way unsteadily to the door while Jack again turned to his aunt.

'Sorry,' he apologised. 'You were in the middle of trying to tell me something.'

Eva returned his gaze with a sick and weary expression.

'Sit down, Jack. There is something I need to tell you.'

And so, he found himself in the same chair that had been occupied by his mother some ten years earlier.

'You see,' began Eva. 'Unlike you, I left school when I was barely ten and started working as a virtual skivvy for a high-class catering firm. They would put on banquets for the lesser royalty and that sort of thing. Believe it or not, my wages were a paltry two and six a week. Anyway,' she continued, 'by the time I was your age, I'd worked my way up to silver service, but, by then, it was obvious that men found me very attractive.'

Jack nodded.

'And you're still a very beautiful lady,' he agreed.

'That's very kind of you,' she said, with a smile, 'but, of course, I'm older now.' Eva dropped her voice. 'My attraction became a trap because at one particularly upper-class gathering – I think it was at Highdown Castle, just north of London – one of the male elite approached me with an indecent proposition.'

Jack didn't take his eyes off her for a moment.

'You must realise,' she stressed, 'that I'd never even seen a ten-shilling note and this man was offering me a hundred pounds if I'd spend the night with him. You know, I can still see the tightly rolled bunch of notes he'd taken from his pocket.'

'And you took it,' Jack said, in a breath.

Eva nodded miserably.

'It was more money than I could earn in ten years. Yes, I took it.' She sighed. 'And I stepped onto the slippery path that leads to damnation.'

'So, you became a bit like King Edward's Lillie Langtry?'

'Well,' she added, quietly, 'I was worse than Langtry, because, as far as I know, she was mistress to just one man, while I...' At that point, her voice trailed off.

'You mean,' finished Jack, 'that you drifted from man to man.'

She rose from her seat to get a cold compress for the bruising on her cheek and it gave her nephew time for some serious thought.

'Anyway,' she continued, after returning and applying the compress to her face, 'word must have got around that I was available at the right price. Six months later, Lord Onslow of Merstrom Towers approached me with the offer of a thousand pounds if I would sleep with him for a week. A thousand pounds!' she exclaimed. 'Can you even begin to imagine it?' She shrugged. 'But money is nothing to men like that. They live in an entirely different world to us.' She shuddered involuntarily. 'It was the most disgusting week of perversions you can imagine, but the money gave me independence and was more than enough to pay for this bungalow.'

Jack had studied her carefully throughout, before finally observing, 'You mean you were a high-class hooker.'

'Yes, to my shame. That's just what I was.'

'But what about the fat man I've just thrown out?'

She raised her eyebrows. 'He obviously hadn't heard that I no longer do that sort of thing and when I made it clear, he got nasty. I'd never personally experienced any violence before, but I knew it was a risk of the game. I'm just glad you came back when you did or goodness only knows what he would have done.'

The room faced west and, by this time, the sun had sunk low in the sky to cast diamond-shaped patterns from the mullion window across the carpeted floor.

'So, what do you think of your aunt now?' she asked in a subdued voice.

Taking her hand, Jack replied, 'All I know is that you've been very good and loving to me. What you've done in your private life...' He shrugged.

'And you, Jack,' she responded, with tears gathering in her eyes, 'have been like the son I never had.'

'Well, we can always pretend,' he suggested, then leaving the room to get his evening meal.

'Yes,' she echoed quietly after he'd gone. 'We can always pretend.'

*

Later that same evening, Jack met Michael in a local pub, which rejoiced in the name of The Toby Jug. Totally different from The Broken Barrel in Wellborn Street, it was both light and spacious.

'There you are, Jack!' exclaimed his companion,

plonking a well-filled tankard on their table. 'Get that down you. It'll put hairs on your chest, as they say.' But then, noticing Jack's hand, he asked, 'What the hell have you done to your knuckles? You're not getting careless with the bacon slicer, I hope.'

Jack smiled and shook his head. 'Nothing like that,' he assured his friend, then proceeded to describe the recent events at his aunt's bungalow.

'Anyway,' he stressed, 'I finally gave the guy a couple of smacks and threw him out.' Michael took a draught from his beer and nodded his approval. He knew nothing of Eva and Jack felt free to vent his feelings. 'She's been wonderful to me, but she's a prostitute. Well, at least until recently. Selling her body for money! It really makes me wonder about women. And then there's me. I'm the result of my mother's adulterous relationship.' He leaned forward, before adding, 'She was actually carrying on an affair while she was married to the man I believed to be my father.'

Then, sitting back, Jack folded his arms and added wearily, 'I don't know, but it's enough to put me off women for life.'

Michael smiled as he put down his drink.

'What you really mean is that it's put you off women for life until you meet the right one.'

Prophetic words, indeed – if they'd ever been uttered.

Chapter 6

THE FOLLOWING DAY saw Jack turning up for work in a sombre and reflective mood.

Seeing his expression, his boss called out.

'I see you've heard then.'

'Sorry, Mr Brownlow,' Jack said, making a start on the bloodstained sawdust floor. 'Heard what?'

'The King's died. Edward passed away early this morning.'

It was Friday 6th May 1910 and subsequent world events would later make Jack wonder if the king had had a lucky escape.

'Well, he was not young when his mother died,' observed Ada's son. 'And no one lives forever.'

Nevertheless, with the king's death, the Edwardian era passed into history and, arguably, a certain graciousness that was never to be quite recovered. The last of Victorian chivalry was gone – an age when ladies wore graceful, long dresses and large floral hats, together with an occasional parasol. It was an age when men would offer them their arm and raise their hat in tribute to their being the weaker sex. It was an age of "after you" and not the "every man for himself" attitude so prevalent in the twentieth century.

Jack's boss turned his attention away from the bacon slicer and asked, 'Did you happen to think any more about the job at the abattoir?'

Jack paused and leaned on his broom.

'I have,' he replied, slowly, 'but, to be honest, I just haven't got it in me to look into the innocent eyes of a lamb and deliver the death blow. I just couldn't do it.'

Barely had he finished speaking when Mrs Simpson came bustling in – with "bustle" being the operative word, for it always formed an outstanding feature of her stylish dress. But what always intrigued Jack was the true size of her diminutive waist once its restraints had been removed.

She fluttered her eyelids.

'Good morning, Jack.'

The woman was obviously an outrageous flirt. In fact, he sometimes doubted the need for the frequency of her visits, but she was closely followed in by an older woman accompanied by a pretty blonde girl in her late teens. Jack knew the lady as Mrs Marshall – a quietly stylish woman who always dropped by on a Friday for the family's weekend joint. Normally, she dealt with Mr Brownlow. However, on this occasion, she made a beeline for Jack, who had just finished the floor.

'Jack,' she began quietly. 'I don't know quite how to put this, but I was wondering if you could do me a favour.' He'd grown to know her quite well over the years and they'd often exchanged a pleasant chat. Moreover, it was this kind of social interaction that had gone a long way over his decision about the abattoir.

The blonde girl held back near the doorway as Jack nodded.

'Well, if there's anything I can do...'

'You see,' began the older woman, in the same quiet voice. 'The girl in the doorway is my daughter.'

After a covert gaze, Jack smiled. 'Pretty girl.'

'Jack,' she said, 'you've always struck me as a decent and honourable young man. Now, the fact is, there's a dance at the Croydon Town Hall tomorrow night and she's desperate to go. It would be her first night out and I was wondering...' She hesitated. 'Well, I was wondering if perhaps you would be kind enough to escort her and keep an eye on things. You know the sort of thing I mean.'

He leaned heavily on his broom.

'Mrs Marshall,' he responded, 'I'd be more than pleased to accompany your daughter – provided, that is, there are no implications. If I'm honest, I'm no great shakes on the dance floor, but I'll certainly keep an eye on her for you.'

'Thank you, Jack. I'm very grateful.' She smiled. 'She's my only daughter so I'm sure you'll understand.'

*

The following evening provided a pleasant surprise for the butcher's assistant, because when he collected

Mrs Marshall's daughter, she looked absolutely stunning. Nearer his own age than he had at first realised, she wore an off-the-shoulder ankle-length blue silk dress with matching net sleeves and top – all of which were enhanced by a naturally slim waist and golden hair – topped by a wide floral hat.

'Wow! You look fantastic,' he exclaimed. 'And I don't even know your name.'

'It's Marian,' she responded in a soft, gentle voice. 'And I know your name's Jack.'

He smiled and nodded, offering her his arm. 'To the ball, Cinderella!' he exclaimed. 'To the ball.'

Once inside the dance hall, they had to fight their way through lines of predatorial men gathered just inside the door to "eye up the available talent", as some of them would put it. Sadly, in a few years' time, many of these same young men were destined to lay stretched out dead on some distant field of conflict.

As Jack had admitted, he was not much on the dance floor. Nevertheless, he did his best to guide Mrs Marshall's daughter round the floor during the first waltz and, when the music stopped, Marian was quick to show her appreciation.

'Why, thank you, Jack,' she said, smiling. 'I really enjoyed that.'

Despite a certain caution, he found himself increasingly drawn to her warm and simple charm.

'Look,' he suggested. 'I'll sit you at that table over there in the corner for a minute while I get you a drink. What would you like? A small sweet sherry perhaps?'

Marian again smiled with a nod and he promised to be right back. However, even during the short time he was away, some opportunist had occupied Jack's seat and was talking earnestly to his protégé. By now, Jack was a good six feet three and weighing in at some fourteen stone plus. He wasted no time.

'Excuse me, old sunshine, but you've taken my place. So, if you don't mind...' And with that, he handed Marian her drink and the interloper, upon seeing the opposition, quickly made himself scarce. 'Blimey!' said Jack, as he settled down with his own drink. 'These vultures don't miss a trick.'

Marian then demonstrated a side of her nature that he was finding increasingly appealing. 'Oh, I don't know,' she said quietly. 'After all, they're only people trying to find the right companion. They're not all after... well, you know what.'

'Possibly,' agreed Jack. 'Possibly. Changing the subject... tell me, what sort of career have you chosen? I bet you're into something like teaching.'

She again smiled one of her warm and frequent smiles.

'I did think about it,' she explained, 'but I felt I could make a greater contribution by becoming a nurse. At the moment, I'm training at Croydon General.'

Jack nodded. 'Very laudable. A very laudable profession!' he exclaimed, finding himself warming to her ever more by the moment.

*

Later that evening and during the last waltz, Jack heard Marian gently whisper his name and, looking down, found himself gazing into her large blue eyes.

'Have you got a regular girlfriend, Jack?' she murmured.

It came at him like a bolt out of the blue and, as he gazed up at the large revolving crystal sphere suspended high above the floor, he found himself at a loss for words. His delay told her all she needed to know, while, in turn, he felt the primeval instinct, present in all men, to crush her in his arms and kiss her, become almost unmanageable.

However, for that particular night, she was his ward and such behaviour would have been unthinkable. So, instead, he maintained the correct dance posture and contented himself with a casual, 'Oh, I know a few young ladies, but nothing serious.'

At the end of the evening, when he dropped her off at Mrs Marshall's, Marian looked up at him with her now familiar and warm smile.

'Thank you for a lovely time, Jack. And thank you for being such a gentleman.' Then, standing on tiptoes, she reached up to kiss him on the cheek, while, high above, the sliver of a brilliant crescent-shaped moon hung in a star-spangled sky. 'A magic moment,' she murmured.

'A magic moment,' Jack echoed softly.

Then, with a final wave, she was gone. Afterwards, Jack stood for a long time on the pavement deep in

41

thought. It would be some time before he saw her again and then it would be under very different circumstances.

Chapter 7

JACK HAD ENJOYED the night out with Marian far more than he would care to admit, even to himself, and yet, somehow, he allowed the time to slip by without seeing her again. It was something he would later bitterly regret. Another four years passed by, but the image of her smile remained as fresh as ever.

But these were not just any four years, because not only had Jack grown into a fully mature twenty-year-old man, but events were developing abroad that would, metaphorically, set the civilised world ablaze and dismantle the established social order for ever.

On the evening of Monday 29th June 1914, Jack met Michael at The Toby Jug, but as Michael placed two well-filled tankards on their table, Jack couldn't help but notice the solemn expression on his pal's face.

'Something on your mind, Michael?' he enquired, taking the first sip of his beer.

'I don't think,' responded his friend, 'that you're quite into foreign affairs like I am, but, the fact is, Archduke Franz Ferdinand was assassinated yesterday afternoon in the Balkans.'

'Archduke who?' began Jack.

'He's the heir – well, he was – to the Austro-Hungarian empire and I'm afraid their alliance with Germany may cause trouble if they retaliate over the murder.'

At that time, it was, of course, guesswork, but it was guesswork destined to become an agonising reality when, on 4th August 1914, Germany's Kaiser Wilhelm II sent his troops crashing down through Belgium and into Northern France. As the grandson of England's Queen Victoria, his expansionist move was probably motivated more by greed and jealousy of the British Empire than any alliance with his southern neighbours. Nevertheless, this aggressive act was to plunge civilised society into the cauldron of the First World War.

After marching through Belgium, the Imperial German Army advanced west to the River Marne where, after a three-day battle with the French and a small British expeditionary force, they were finally pushed back to the Aisne River. However, the German troops had badly shaken the Western world, not least of which were the two young friends who met regularly in The Toby Jug.

It was Jack's turn to buy the rounds and, handing Michael his pint, he sighed as he sat down.

'I can see why you're concerned about overseas affairs!' he exclaimed. 'If we're not careful, the bloody Krauts will be over here.'

Michael took a long draught from his tankard.

'I'm so concerned,' he emphasised, leaning his chair back on two legs and stretching out his endless frame, 'that I'm going to join up tomorrow.'

For a long moment, Jack studied his friend. 'You mean you're willing to risk your life for a country you've never even visited and know nothing about?'

'They're people, Jack,' Michael protested. 'Like you and me. And so many innocent citizens have lost their lives during the Germans' advance through Belgium. Is that what we really want here? Anyway...' He sighed. 'That's what I intend to do tomorrow.'

'And I,' stressed Jack, 'will be right beside you.'

'Good on you, Jack. Good on you,' said his friend, smiling. For several moments, it fell quiet, before Michael finally came up with a surprising question. 'Did you, by any chance, ever see more of that blonde girl you took to the Croydon dance?'

'That was years ago!' exclaimed Jack. 'How did you come to know about her?'

Michael smiled.

'You obviously didn't notice me, but, like most of the other guys, I was there on the pull.'

Jack grinned, shaking his head. 'No, I haven't seen her and I sometimes wish I had, because she was a lovely, gentle person.' He shrugged. 'But life and all that – you know. In any case, she's probably married by now and I'm never likely to see her again.'

On both of these counts, Jack couldn't have been further from the truth.

*

45

The next morning saw the two young men standing in a line of potential recruits. Finally, it was Michael's turn.

'Name?' snapped the recruiting officer.

'Miles. Michael Miles,' replied Jack's friend.

'Age?' continued the inquisitor in the same irritable tone.

And so it went on until Ada's son stepped up to the desk, which kickstarted the whole process all over again.

'Name?'

'Jack,' he responded.

The official, who was obviously an impatient individual, threw down his pen in exasperation.

'Jack, what? For heaven's sake man! I can't just put down "Jack".'

But he'd shown his impatience with the wrong man and the volunteer's eyes narrowed. 'I said, Jack. And that is what I meant.'

However, if the interviewer hadn't recognised the warning signs, Michael had – and fearing what his friend might do, he quickly stepped forward.

'This man,' he explained, 'has no known father and has, therefore, only ever gone by the name of Jack. You can put his surname down as Miles, because he's effectively my adopted brother.'

*

Later that evening, while standing at the bar of their local, Jack placed both hands on his friend's

46

shoulders and nodded. The gesture really made any words irrelevant, but as he patted Michael's upper arms, he murmured, 'You've been a great friend ever since schooldays. No man could ask for more. And today, well...' At that point, words failed him.

*

Early the following morning, Jack sat opposite his aunt in the lounge of her bungalow and told her of his decision.

'But surely,' protested Eva, 'haven't we got a regular army without you risking your life?' She added, a touch sadly, 'You know, Jack. I've grown very fond of you and, if I'm honest, I'll miss you terribly.'

Jack reached across and took her hand.

'And you, Eva, have been like a mother to me, but look – we'll soon kick the kaiser out of France and I'll back before you know it.'

But the kaiser was not so willing to be kicked out of France and it cost millions of young lives on both sides and five years of bitter fighting before it could be achieved. When Jack left the next day for the local military training centre, he wondered if it would be the last time he'd ever see his aunt or her bungalow again.

Chapter 8

BY LATE OCTOBER 1914, Jack and his friend had undergone three months of extensive military training. Both men had proved to be outstanding and capable soldiers so, by the time they had been posted to the south coast in readiness for transport to Europe, they had each achieved the rank of sergeant.

In those far-off days, it was mandatory for residents on the south coast to provide accommodation for servicemen before they embarked for the Western Front. It was a process that could take months and it was during this time that Jack experienced a life-changing encounter.

The technical term for military accommodation was "billeting" and Jack had been allocated to a family home in a narrow back street of Portslade, just west of Brighton in Sussex. Already a victim of long marches, he anticipated the far greater distances that would be involved once he reached Europe and determined that his boots would need to be comfortable. It was a comparatively minor consideration, but one that was to have major implications. And so it was, he found himself outside a little shoe shop at the corner of his road.

Upon entering, he was immediately greeted by the pungent smell of freshly cut leather and boot polish. In the dimly lit interior, he could make out rows of shelves all neatly stacked and labelled with parcels of newly repaired shoes.

The young female assistant was already busy with another customer, so he had no alternative but to wait his turn. After idly glancing around the shop at the artefacts of the trade, his attention returned to the girl behind the counter. It was at that point he began to realise how graceful and beautiful she was.

Jack was approaching twenty-three and had the same appetite as most young men of his age, but it was an appetite that had been coloured by the adulterous behaviour of his mother and the confession of prostitution by his aunt. All in all, it had made him wary of the fair sex.

However, when the shop assistant finally became free and he found himself gazing into her deep-brown eyes, he knew he had found someone special – someone *very* special. His aunt had been an attractive woman, but this was something different, for, with her heart-shaped face and full cupid-bow lips, she was nothing less than stunning.

The young woman instinctively brushed aside some of her abundant auburn hair. Parted in the middle, it hung down past her shoulders in thick tresses with wisps that tended to stray across her face. For a brief moment after she'd asked if she could be of assistance, Jack was lost for words.

In turn, the young woman found herself confronted by a tall, uniformed stranger, who cut a striking figure with the brass insignia of the Queen's Regiment on his cap and the sergeant's chevrons on his arms. So much so that she unwittingly allowed her gaze to linger for just that second too long. It was a rare and precious moment, one that Jack would carry with him all through his first year in the trenches. However, the dynamics of this catalyst were abruptly shattered by the entry of a man through the rear shop door. Heavily moustached and wearing a stained cobbler's apron, he immediately sensed the atmosphere and ordered the girl back into the house. Thickly built and an obvious bully, the newcomer turned a baleful eye on Jack.

'I should tell you, soldier!' he exclaimed aggressively. 'That girl happens to be my daughter and is barely seventeen, so I wouldn't want you to get any wrong ideas.' Then, squaring up to the sergeant with his full six feet, he added, 'So, I hope, for your sake, I make myself abundantly clear.'

However, the man had no means of knowing what he was dealing with – that Jack was not the type to be intimidated and that he was lucky not to have ended up on the floor of his shop with a bruised jawbone.

Jack studied the speaker carefully and began to wonder how such a brute could have fathered so lovely a daughter. Thick, bushy eyebrows combined with deep frown lines served to convey a perpetually angry scowl, while the high colour of his cheeks spoke of drink.

Jack retorted, 'Be careful, old man, that you don't take on more than you can handle.' As he slowly turned to leave, he again caught a brief glimpse of that something special in the assistant's eyes as she re-entered the shop.

Once outside, he paused to gaze along the busy narrow street. Alive with handcarts and horse-drawn vehicles, it was obviously a very run-down area – a fact evidenced by children running about barefoot. He looked up at the cramped little windows above the shoe shop where he assumed the young girl lived and suddenly realised he didn't even know her name. In fact, he hadn't even had a chance to speak to her. Yet one thing was certain – he would never forget those beautiful eyes and the gentle sound of her voice. He knew the odds were stacked against him with her difficult father and their age difference, but he knew she was the one. From that moment on, he determined to make her his own.

Chapter 9

HOWEVER, BEFORE THERE was even a chance of seeing her again, he was called to France where he experienced the horrors of war for the first time. And in the late January of 1915, he received a deep shrapnel wound high in his left shoulder, with the result that he was repatriated to England for a month's recuperation. Once again, Jack found himself outside the little shoe shop on the corner of what he now knew to be North Street.

On this occasion, the weather was appalling with freezing pavements that lay under a foot of snow. Squinting up into the fast-falling flakes, he knew this might be his only chance to talk to the girl who had seemed so special. Tens of thousands of men had already died in the French campaign and he knew his own chances of surviving the war were, at best, poor. He was also aware of the absolute necessity to avoid another confrontation with the girl's father, so seeing a group of children playing on the opposite pavement, he beckoned for one of them to come across.

'Son, how would you like to earn half a crown?'

he offered, noticing how thin and ill-equipped the boy looked for such bitter conditions.

'Sure, mister,' he replied eagerly. 'What's it for?'

Jack indicated the shoe shop. 'I'd like to know when the man who lives there is most likely to be out.'

The lad had a ready answer. 'You mean the old bloke with a moustache, mister? That's easy, because he's always down the boozer directly as it opens.' And he graphically gesticulated the rhythmic downing of an imaginary pint. 'What's more, 'e don't get back till late. I should know 'cos I've 'eard 'is old woman going on about it.'

*

As a result of this exchange, the following day saw Jack waiting on the pavement opposite the little shop and covertly watching the entrance while apparently reading a newspaper. Sure enough, just as the boy had predicted, the girl's father left right on the hour. Then, waiting to let him get well clear, the soldier entered the shop.

There were no other customers on this occasion and when the assistant looked up and recognised him, the warmth of her smile made everything worthwhile.

'You remember me then!' exclaimed the sergeant with equal warmth.

Obviously embarrassed by her own enthusiasm, the young woman momentarily dropped her gaze before peering up with a determined expression.

'Yes, I do remember you. In fact, I have often remembered you.'

As he once again looked into her stunning brown eyes and at her beautiful face, he felt the same surge of magic all over again. For a moment, they were both lost for words. Finally, however, Jack broke the silence.

'I wondered,' he began tentatively, 'if perhaps I might tempt you out for a late lunch. I understand Mrs Trill has a little tea shop just round the corner in the high street.'

'I'd love to,' she began, 'but... no, wait. I'll ask my sister if she'll mind the shop for a bit – just as long as it doesn't take too much time.' When the sergeant saw the girl's sibling, he found it difficult to tell them apart and the new arrival could scarcely take her eyes off him. 'By the way,' smiled the first girl, 'my name's Lilly and this is my younger sister, Daisy. I know we look alike,' she said, with a grin, 'but in case you get confused, remember it's me you're taking out.'

Daisy, however, was obviously not the inhibited sort.

'Lucky old you!' she exclaimed. 'Where did you manage to dig him up from?'

To which, and not without humour himself, the sergeant dryly observed, 'Well, in my profession, I just hope it doesn't come to that.'

Once in the freezing conditions outside, Jack quickly became aware of the flimsiness of Lilly's coat and immediately removed his military greatcoat before draping it round her shoulders. North Street ran east to west and formed a vortex for what had now become a raging blizzard, which made them only too glad to reach the shelter of their destination. Not that it was luxurious. It wasn't.

Consisting of half a dozen tables adorned with what were originally white cloths, it tended to convey an overall air of drear, while flimsy fly-blown net curtains did little to help. Even the spider's web so carefully crafted at the corner of the window contained a leggy predator too lethargic to consume its prey – although it might have been the intense cold that inhibited the insect, because the funnel-shaped oil heaters had made little impression on the fern-shaped icicles clinging to the inside of the glass.

Apart from themselves, there was only one other patron. Crouched over a cup of tea and with a curved pipe in his mouth, he seemed lost in a world of his own. What actually grabbed Jack's attention was the man's immense white beard, which almost reached the tabletop.

'Blimey!' Jack exclaimed. 'Santa's early this year.'

'Sssh. He'll hear you,' hissed Lilly, as Jack helped her out of his greatcoat.

As she smiled her gratitude, her sudden close proximity and feminine alure proved too much for Jack and, taking her in his arms, he kissed her passionately.

'Err, excuse me,' came the sound of a woman's reedy voice, 'but this happens to be a restaurant, not a petting shop.'

Breaking away, Jack turned to find himself

looking at probably the smallest woman he'd ever seen.

Standing at barely five feet and with thin grey hair parted in the middle, she was, to say the least, an unusual sight, while her whole persona was completed by rimless glasses that she had to constantly adjust on her nose. She was obviously the proprietor and went on to ask about their requirements.

The sergeant looked at Lilly and grimaced.

'Well,' he responded, 'it depends what you have on offer.'

'Beans,' parroted the woman. 'Beans on toast, beans and fried egg, beans and...'

'Oh, beans on toast will be fine,' said Lilly, feeling slightly embarrassed.

*

Jack's month of leave flew by until, suddenly it seemed, it was time to say goodbye to the girl he had grown to love. They tried to see each other as often as possible, but, with the ever-present shadow of her father, it had not been easy. Lilly had desperately wanted to see him off from Portsmouth, but it had not proved possible.

On the last night of his leave and with the ogre safely ensconced in the local pub, the sergeant paid a final visit.

'Oh, Jack,' pleaded Lilly, holding him close. 'Please be careful.'

'I promise,' he assured her. 'I really promise. And when I come back...'

He went on to describe the future he had planned for them.

Finally, but finally, it was time to go and, with a lingering parting of hands, Jack stepped back out into the freezing snow.

Chapter 10

WHEN THE SERGEANT got off the train in France to rejoin his regiment, it was to a scene of utter devastation, for he was faced with a landscape fought over by two powerful opposing armies with all the destructive capability of mechanised warfare. Shattered and roofless buildings lay on every side, while stumps that had once been trees pointed their splintered remains forlornly towards the sky – almost, as it were, in a plaintiff cry of agony and confusion. Fields were indistinguishable one from the other, pockmarked by numerous craters and with hedgerows that had long been torn apart. They had born mute witness to the violence that had passed over them.

And then there were the graves. Dug at random, the sad mounds represented the end of a dream – not only for their occupants, but for those who had been left behind. They served as a grim reminder of the sergeant's own vulnerability.

Flashes of bright light on the horizon and the continual crackle of distant gunfire signalled the ongoing conflict. It caused Jack to remember the lines of a lament so often sung in the trenches.

I want to go home, I want to go home
I don't want to go in the trenches no more
Where whizz bangs and shrapnel they whistle
  and roar
Take me over the sea, where the Alleyman can't
  get at me
Oh my, I don't want to die, I want to go home

Several months after the sergeant had returned to the front line, rumour became rife of a huge push all along the River Somme. And so, on the 1st July 1916, at 7.30am precisely, the whole fifteen-mile-long British front line opened fire with its heavy artillery. The Battle of the Somme had begun. Salvo after salvo was sent smashing into the German positions in an endless torrent of high explosives. Huge geysers of earth and debris erupted into the sky, with the ground shaking under the immense impact of each shell, while deep in the trenches of the opposing British Army, soldiers winced at the intensity of the maelstrom.

At this stage of the offensive, the pressures were very much on the gunners as they sprang to reload after the ejection of each spent cartridge. However, they soon found themselves firing into a distant fog as the enemy's emplacements became obscured by great clouds of drifting dust and cordite smoke. Gone was the early morning beauty of the blue summer sky. The plains surrounding the Somme area had become embroiled into a manmade hell. The theory had been that nothing could withstand such an onslaught. That had been the theory. Soon, the rhythmic onslaught ceased and was replaced by an eerie silence.

Crouched in their trenches, the steel-helmeted British Tommies awaited the signal to leave the safety of their dugouts and advance across no man's land.

'Sergeant, excuse me.' The speaker was a short but stocky Welsh corporal from the valleys – a man with a ready smile and a glass-half-full attitude to life. 'Sorry to trouble you,' he continued, looking up at Jack, 'but a lot of the men are scared of going over the top.'

'We're all scared,' responded the sergeant, 'but unless we want German jackboots stalking all over our green and pleasant land, we've no alternative.'

'We understand that, Sergeant,' replied the corporal, nodding.

'Now,' exclaimed his superior, 'tell the men to fix their bayonets and be ready to follow me up the ladders. Let's give the enemy a taste of British steel.'

In reality, it was German lead that would carry the day.

Finally, the reed-like whistles sounded all along the line and, in response, a river of khaki poured out of the earth into the vacuousness of no man's land.

As he glanced along the corridors of men as they spread out, Jack caught sight of Michael and his lieutenant in front of their platoon. Raising a hand in greeting, he was immediately rewarded with a vigorous thumbs-up sign. However, it was sadly destined to be the last contact they would ever have.

Then, as the tide of men started to move forward, the insane chattering of the enemy machine guns began to reap its terrible human harvest. It seemed that someone would cry out and crumple into the long grass almost every second. Whatever confidence the British military authorities had placed on the effectiveness of their barrage, it was proving catastrophically wrong, for the enemy had been virtually inviolate in their underground cities of defence and immediately the shells ceased falling they had emerged to man their gun emplacements. If the English had been lax in their foresight, the same could not be said of the enemy. Salient dugouts had been positioned far out from their front line and afforded murderous crossfire curtains of flying lead.

Jack had scant time to dwell on the unfolding horror before a hammer-like blow struck the side of his head and caused his brain to reel from the clamouring inside his helmet. Falling to the ground, he felt his Lee-Enfield rifle fly from his hand as though it had a life of its own.

How long he lay in a semi-conscious state, he had no idea, but, finally, when awareness returned, the sun had become low in the sky. His rifle lay nearby with its butt splintered to matchwood, which, he suspected, together with the protection of his helmet, had probably saved his life. His left shoulder, however, hurt – ironically, the same shoulder that had been injured by shrapnel. However, on this occasion, a bullet had caused the damage and his tunic was soaked with blood.

Glancing around while struggling to his feet, Jack became appalled by the numerous casualties that littered the ground. A few feet to his right lay the body of his happy-go-lucky corporal. Lying on his back, the Welshman was gazing up at the sky with eyes that could no longer see. The machine guns had fallen silent. With the exception of a crack of a sniper's rifle, all was quiet.

At first, Jack wondered if he imagined it, but then, after listening more carefully, he could just make out a feeble voice calling for help. The cry seemed to emanate from a shell crater still further to his right and, glancing over its rim, he caught sight of an officer lying on the ground with one leg twisted unnaturally behind his body. He was obviously an older man and Jack could see from his insignia that he held the rank of major. As he approached, he saw something that completely obliterated anything else from his mind, for a deep and vivid scar ran from the corner of the officer's forehead to the bridge of his nose.

Suddenly, the sergeant was six again and back in his old home in Wellborn Street with his father's words still ringing in his ears. 'It'll be the last time he'll be so keen to violate someone else's marriage, because I've smashed a glass tankard over the bastard's head.'

And the stark reality that this man was probably his real father proved almost too much, for although Jack owed his very existence to the officer, the man had also destroyed his home life and indirectly robbed him of his mother.

Grabbing the officer by the lapels, Jack demanded to know his name, but, already in agony, the major could barely speak.

'Your name?' the sergeant almost screamed. 'Your name!'

'Major... Major Van der Berg,' came the tortured reply.

Far off, the crackle of gunfire could still just about be heard and somehow seemed to reflect the drama of the moment and Jack's agonising dilemma – the dilemma as to whether, in his weakened state, to try and get the officer back to the British lines or leave him to an almost certain death from his wounds and the cold of the oncoming night.

Finally, however, Jack's conscience prevailed, but as he lifted the officer to his feet, the injured man cried out in pain. His right leg was useless and Jack had to carry virtually his entire weight. It took every ounce of his depleted strength and how he made it back to their own lines, he would never know.

*

Field hospitals, or dressing stations as they were known, were often situated not far behind the front line and frequently took the form of a requisitioned farmhouse. Most of them were, by necessity, very basic and often vermin-ridden, with only their basements affording any real protection, while the bare and dirty brickwork cellar spaces proved quite inadequate for the vast flood of victims pouring in from that first fatal day of engagement.

Limited light emanated from grubby hurricane lamps, which were interspersed along low, soot-blackened ceilings. In this flickering half-dark atmosphere, it was possible to make out row after row of wounded men either lying on the floor or on blood-soaked cots. The shadowy figures of nurses moved about their damage-limitation work – although, despite their best efforts, the dusty air frequently echoed with the piercing cries of the wounded.

Distant gunfire proved a constant irritation, while the buildings themselves would shake from the occasional shell burst. It was in such an atmosphere that the sergeant finally found himself.

'Jack,' called a somehow familiar voice. 'Is that really you?'

Turning on his side, Ada's son saw an attractive blonde nurse. However, this was no ordinary nurse, but a face from the past. Unable to believe his eyes, Jack struggled upright.

'Marian! What on earth are you doing in this hellhole?'

Older now, she had matured into a beautiful woman and the sergeant felt a pang of regret – regret that he had never followed up their first date.

She sat down gingerly on the edge of his cot, ignoring his question, and murmured wistfully, 'I never forgot you, Jack, and I always hoped that we'd meet again someday, but not like this.'

He studied her for a moment, with her blonde hair beneath the nurse's cape. Her gentle way of speaking made him realise how natural it would have been to take her in his arms – but then there was Lilly. Jack felt emotionally torn, but suddenly the cellar vibrated from the massive impact of a nearby explosion, which brought clouds of dust raining down on the victims below. An agonising cry of pain quickly brought Marian to her feet.

'Back in a minute,' she promised, and as the sergeant watched her trim figure disappear into the murk, he wondered about the irony of life.

Suddenly, however, Jack noticed a tall, lean man with a blood-soaked head bandage making his way towards his cot.

'Lance Corporal Simms!' exclaimed the sergeant, as he recognised the newcomer. 'So, you made it.'

Quite the reverse of Jack's lance corporal, Simms was a dour, quiet man.

'Yes, Sarge. I was lucky. A bullet hit my helmet and knocked me cold.' He shrugged. 'I don't know if you heard, but there's only two of us left.' The lean man looked grimy and dishevelled. 'The whole platoon!' he exclaimed bitterly. 'Gone – and for what?'

'And Sergeant Miles' platoon?' prompted Jack.

'All dead, I'm afraid,' he explained. 'Well, except for four and they're in the next cellar with me – though I doubt whether two of them will make it.'

'And Sergeant Miles...?'

But the lance corporal shook his head.

'I'm sorry, Sarge. We all knew you were buddies – but there's one slight consolation. They managed to retrieve his body. Most of the dead are still out there. It's just too dangerous to do anything about it.'

Devastated by the news of his old school friend, Jack swung his legs over the side of his cot.

'I suppose you don't happen to know when the burial squads start work?'

'I'm not sure, Sarge.'

Before he could finish, the cellar rocked again under the shock of a nearby explosion.

'The burial squads?' persisted Jack.

'Around daybreak I would imagine, Sarge. Why do you ask?'

Without replying, the ex-butcher reached for his tunic. Although desperately weak, he determined to do right by his friend. However, alarmed by Jack's obvious unsteadiness, the NCO moved to intervene, only to be unceremoniously brushed aside as Ada's son made his way to the exit staircase. Upon reaching the top, he became aware of a frantic voice from behind.

'Jack! Jack!' came Marian's voice. 'Wait till it's dark. There's a German sniper zeroed in on that doorway.'

Even as she spoke, there came the distant and vicious crack of a rifle, and the sergeant felt a bullet zip past his head like an angry wasp. Then, to his horror, this was followed by the sickening sound of it hitting flesh. Turning, he was just in time to hear the nurse gasp, before she tumbled backwards onto the basement floor, before laying in a silent and crumpled heap.

'No. No!' shouted Jack as he raced to her side, only to see an ever-widening crimson stain on the front of her uniform. While bending down to lift her up by the shoulders, she looked at him with eyes that were fast misting over.

'Oh, Jack,' she whispered. 'I could so have loved you.' She paused before coughing flecks of blood, then added in a fading voice, 'Only now, it's too late.' With that, she sighed gently as her chin dropped on to her chest.

'Marian!' urged the sergeant desperately. 'It's not too late.'

A medic stooped to feel her pulse and, looking at Jack, shook his head.

'I'm sorry,' he murmured sadly, 'but I'm afraid that whatever the lady had in mind really is too late.'

Jack took her in his arms and held her close for a long time, all the while agonising over the meaninglessness of life. He looked at the medic, who had remained hunkered down by his side.

'What kind of world are we in?' cried the devastated sergeant. 'A beautiful person like this and suddenly gone.'

His mind slipped back to the night they had danced together and he remembered so vividly how full of life and energy she had been, her shining happy eyes, and how she'd always been eager for the next waltz. Her whole life in front of her. And now...

How bitterly he wished he'd followed up on their first date – although would it have altered their destiny?

The whole situation left the sergeant in a quandary, for while not wishing to leave Marian in such miserable circumstances, he was desperate to reach the burial pits and lay his friend to rest before it was too late.

Now wary of the deadly marksman and despite his injured arm, Jack crawled lizard-like away from the top of the stairwell. Maintaining a reptilian movement, he eventually found it a relief to be in the open air after the stifling atmosphere of the cellar.

Little remained above basement level of what once had been a comfortable family house. Devastated walls gave scant indication of its original appearance or, indeed, any information of the people who had once called it home. Its few remaining rafters, devoid of any tiles, clawed skywards in a splintered agony, but the sergeant had little time or inclination to dwell on the personal tragedies of those who might have been involved. After dragging his way over piles of bricks and broken household artefacts, he at last felt it safe to stand up and make his way to the burial pits.

Finally, he was on the road that led to his goal – yawning black chasms in the ground that screamed their silent and ghastly purpose. However, seeing the duty squad in action made him immediately wonder if he wasn't already too late. He approached the lieutenant in charge.

'Yes, Sergeant. What is it?' came the curt response

from behind a trim moustache and a façade of well-tailored khaki uniform.

Jack, who had put the man's age at barely twenty-one, attempted to explain the purpose of his mission.

'I understand, sir,' he said, respectfully, 'that some of those killed in yesterday's advance have been recovered. And I wondered whether my friend, Sergeant Miles, was among them.'

Standing to a martinet-like attention, the slightly younger man gave no immediate indication that he'd even heard, but, instead, looked Jack up and down with obvious disdain. The half-buttoned tunic slung loosely around Jack's shoulders, together with his unshaven face, was obviously at odds with the lieutenant's sense of military protocol and he was quick to acidly point out the discrepancies.

'Sergeant,' he snapped, 'your appearance is a disgrace. Straighten up and button your uniform correctly. NCOs are meant to be an example of self-respect and discipline. That, Sergeant, is the bedrock of military discipline. I might also ask by whose authority you have absented yourself from your platoon. It looks to me as if you are in gross dereliction of your duties – and, I might add, in danger of a court martial.'

Jack quietly studied the speaker with an unwavering gaze before replying, sarcastically, 'Platoon, sir? What platoon? Don't you know they're all dead? Our leaders, you see, sir, got it wrong. Terribly, terribly wrong. And after yesterday's blunder, there's hardly a platoon left.'

The sergeant knew he was being insubordinate, but from the lieutenant's sanctimonious attitude, he was obviously probably part of a new draft of officers from Sandhurst and knew little or nothing of the first day's nightmare on the Somme.

Nevertheless, boiling with anger and despite the pain of his wound, Jack took a step forward to stare the officer straight in the face. Towering over the smaller man, he didn't mince his words.

'Just be thankful, sir,' he hissed, 'that you're in that uniform. And pray to God you never meet me in civvy street. Now, sir, I'll ask you again. Is Sergeant Miles waiting here for burial? And if so – where?'

In the First World War, men had been shot for less, but the lieutenant just blanched and, although obviously shaken, endeavoured to retain some semblance of composure.

'I suppose, Sergeant, you realise I could have you arrested?'

But Jack was unrepentant. 'You think so, sir!' he exclaimed, opening his tunic to reveal swathes of bandages. 'Do you really believe anyone would take you seriously? I doubt it.' He looked around. 'There are no witnesses. It's just between you and me, lieutenant, sir.'

Inexperienced and young, the officer felt at an increasing loss and glanced down at the clipboard in his left hand. 'Sergeant Miles has been allocated to pit five,' he explained, in a subdued voice.

Without bothering to reply, Jack turned on his heels to make his way towards the specified area

– an area where sad rows of parcelled bodies lay patiently awaiting their interment. Upon seeing Jack's sergeant's chevrons, the nearest orderly immediately snapped to attention and saluted. Then, after hearing the purpose of his mission, the orderly led him to the far side of the pit where he was shown the mortal remains of his friend, who was now nothing more than an inert package ready for disposal.

He remembered that first day they had met in the junior school playground and how, between them, they had trounced the Jack Sprat teasing. He thought of the many times they had shared a drink together at The Toby Jug. Friends for life – or so it had seemed, for now it was all too early to say goodbye.

Although there was a slight drizzle, the previous night had witnessed a heavy downpour and turned the whole area into a quagmire, which had caused the clay at the pit edge to become slippery and dangerous. The sergeant, still weak from his wound, would have lost his footing had it not been for the speedy reaction of the orderly.

'Look, Sergeant,' he urged as he supported Jack's arm, 'you're in no state to do this alone. Why don't you at least let me take the main weight of your friend? We can lay him to rest between us.' He looked sympathetically at the sergeant. 'I appreciate why you're doing this and I'm sure he'd understand.'

Jack returned the man's gaze and nodded. 'I must admit, I could use the help.'

Even with the orderly's assistance, the sergeant

was hard put to maintain his balance as they negotiated the descent. Ankle-deep in mud, it seemed a desolate place to leave his friend. After reverently laying Michael alongside his comrades, Jack straightened up and bowed his head.

'Goodbye, old friend. Thanks for all the good times we shared together. I hate to leave you here, but I promise you, if I survive this hell, I'll do my best to live a life for both of us. I owe you that much.' With that, the sergeant turned away, his eyes blinded by tears.

'What are we doing to each other?' queried the orderly as he helped the sergeant out of the trench. 'Thousands of men killed yesterday – in a matter of minutes – and for what? A few feet of bloody ground that's not even England.'

Bowed with weariness from the pain in his wound, Jack tried to formulate some sort of response.

'Funny,' he replied, finally. 'I asked someone a similar question earlier today and, the fact is, we're doing things our way.' Jack shrugged before adding, 'And this is the result. My advice is: don't do too much thinking. Just do your duty and hope to survive.'

Chapter 11

LATER THAT EVENING, in the dim light of the cellar, Jack found it hard to sleep. In the past twenty-four hours, he'd lost two very important people in his life. And although Michael and he had been very close, it was Marian's unexpected re-entry into his life that had been most disturbing.

Sleep came slowly and almost imperceptibly, and he began to dream – although whether it was a dream or reality would become difficult to determine, for he found himself in a beautiful, wooded glade. It might have been an orchard, as fruit abounded on every side. Grapes grew in thick bunches that clung to a distant wall and then there was the light. So brilliant, yet so gentle. However, what puzzled Jack was the absence of shadows, while, glancing up at the clear and tranquil blue sky, he could see no sign of the sun. The light, it appeared, was self-perpetuating. Moreover, as he continued to glance about, he was totally overcome by a sense of absolute peace. Wherever it was, it was a far cry from the hell he'd left behind.

As he roamed through the serene glades, he came

upon something that stopped him dead in his tracks, for there, under a blossom-laden tree, was Marian – not quite as he remembered her, for she looked absolutely radiant. Her long hair shone and she was clad in a spotless white dress tied at the waist by a band that matched her hair. She looked totally happy and appeared to be skipping with a woman about her own age – a woman that Jack could have sworn was a younger version of her mother, Mrs Simpson.

Suddenly, however, Marian appeared to catch sight of the sergeant. 'Jack,' she called out. 'Please don't be sad about me. I'm perfectly fine.'

In the distance, he thought he caught a glimpse of Michael laughing and joking with another man – although, even in the clear pure air, they were so far away he couldn't be sure.

Then, as he made his way towards Marian, he was surprised when she recoiled.

'Jack,' she whispered. 'I could have so loved you, but it's not possible here – in the physical sense.'

Even as she spoke, the images began to fade – although he couldn't be sure whether they were receding or if it was him drawing back into reality.

As he awoke to a pain on the side of his face, he found himself looking into the two closely set, beady black eyes of a rat.

The sharp-faced rodent had been busy peering over the edge of Jack's bedcover and was gnawing at his face. The sergeant was no stranger to vermin. He had shared the trenches with them, they had gnawed at his uniform and even stolen the food from his tin plate, but this was too much – and although it is not in the remit of this account to describe subsequent events, sufficient to say Jack ensured the creature would cause no further problems.

With the rodent disposed of, Jack lay awake for a long time trying to decide whether he'd experienced a wishful dream or something more tangible. Had he, by whatever means, been privileged with a glance into the hereafter? It was something he would query many times – particularly in the light of future tragic events.

Chapter 12

WHILE JACK HAD been undergoing the ordeal of interring his friend, a quite different drama had been unfolding back in the home of his beloved Lilly. Her father – the bullying moustached cobbler – had always relied on his little shoe shop for the livelihood of his family and income had recently been greatly enhanced by a contract with the army.

However, this had become a mixed blessing for it had made him complacent and he had neglected his regular customers. Worse, his heavy drinking had eroded his profits and financial ruin was looming. One night, in the single back room behind the shop, Sarah, his wife, sat him down and laid out some home truths.

'Isaac!' she exclaimed. 'If you don't take the financial situation seriously, we'll end up on the street.'

She and her husband had been married for some twenty years and it had not been an easy time. She had sacrificed a career in education to be with him, thereby making them solely dependent upon his skills as a shoesmith. He leaned back in his chair with folded thick forearms.

'I don't see why,' he retorted, stroking his prodigious moustache. 'We've got the army contract.'

'Can't you see?' she shouted angrily. 'This war won't go on forever and then what? The fact is, Isaac, you're lazy and waste too much money on booze.'

*

Three days after this remonstration, the axe fell and due to his falling so far behind with the army work, the government cancelled his contract. Sarah angrily confronted her husband again.

'Now what? Where do we go from here? How do we pay the rent and feed the children? I might also add, in case you hadn't noticed, our Beulah is far from well.'

It is relevant to note that in 1917 there was no social welfare for poverty-stricken families. It was a stark choice between the street and the workhouse.

Even as she spoke, the sound of a racking cough could be heard from the room overhead. Sarah looked despairingly at her husband.

'If I'm not mistaken, that's tuberculosis.'

Beulah had always been the frail one of the three girls.

'I'll get Doctor Wilson to drop in and see her first thing in the morning,' responded Isaac.

'And how do you propose paying him?' shouted his wife. 'With one of your spare rubber heels, perhaps?'

'Oh, Doctor Wilson's a good man. He won't want his money straightaway.'

'Huh! That's if he gets it at all,' Sarah muttered under her breath.

But the doctor was a philanthropist and would often waive his medical fees. It kept him poor, but all rewards don't necessarily come in the form of financial renumeration. Fortunately, Doctor Wilson was one such man. However, even philanthropists can't work miracles and, as he descended their rickety staircase accompanied by the sound of Beulah's racking cough, he looked solemn.

He was not a tall man by any standards and, though into middle life, he retained a thick head of hair – which was now quite white. His midriff, however, had managed to get completely out of control, as his waistcoat buttons bore mute testimony. A Gladstone bag completed his medical persona. Entering the small living room, he was confronted by Lilly, who had just come in from the shop.

'My sister will be alright, won't she?' she pleaded.

'You know,' responded the physician, 'it's not always easy being a doctor. I wish I could say the things that loved ones wanted to hear.' He paused while removing the stethoscope from around his neck and snapped it shut before putting it in his bag. 'The fact is that's not always possible.' Then, sitting down, he looked at Sarah. 'The truth is,' he said, bluntly, 'your daughter has advanced tuberculosis of the lungs and we have no known cure.'

'You mean...' cried her mother.

'I'm afraid so. Yes. Good food, if you can afford it, would help, but in the long term... There is, however,' he added, 'the option of Foredown Isolation Hospital. The germs don't like the cold air of the Downs.' He shrugged. 'But it's a contagious place and the downside would be the problem of visiting her. It's a difficult decision and one that only you can make.' He reached into his bag and withdrew a medicine bottle containing a thick brown fluid. 'When the coughing gets too bad,' he advised, 'give her a tablespoon full of that. It will ease the soreness.'

*

Long after the doctor had left, a pall of gloom hung over the small room.

'Well, one thing's certain, no daughter of mine is going to be left to die in some hospital,' Sarah said adamantly. She turned to her husband. 'Isaac, you heard what the doctor said. Our daughter must have the best of everything. And that means you getting down to some hard work.'

The cobbler was absolutely shattered by the news and, uncharacteristically, got to his feet without a word, before making his way through to their small shop. Lilly and her sister Daisy had been reduced to absolute silence, while Sarah – a mother among mothers – tenderly put her arms round them.

'You know,' she said gently. 'None of us are here forever. And if the good Lord choses to take our Beulah, then who knows what suffering she may be spared? In the meantime, we'll do our best to make her comfortable and happy. And, above all, we must show her how much she's loved. Never, *never*,' she emphasised, 'let her see us looking sad.'

*

Later in the day, Sarah happened to notice a folded newspaper lying under the table. She assumed the doctor had dropped it accidentally and reached to pick it up. It was a copy of *The Illustrated London News*, dated 17th July 1916, and the headlines made for stark reading.

The Cost of a Day on the Somme

Anxiously, she scanned the seemingly endless columns of dead, fearful that she might find the name of her eldest son, who had been conscripted into the cavalry. However, to her immense relief, he was not listed. However, she caught sight of something that made her catch her breath, for there was a name she recognised only too well – Sergeant Jack Miles. It seemed the final straw.

Sarah was in a far from enviable position. Married at seventeen to a lazy brute of a man, she had been worried sick by the outbreak of war knowing that her two sons were eligible for military service. And the news of Beulah had devastated her, for tuberculosis was a highly contagious disease and could easily spread through her entire family. In addition, Lilly had confided her love for Sergeant Jack and their plans for the future, so now she had the added mental burden of keeping the news of his death to herself or breaking her daughter's heart with the truth.

However, time moves on and, although Beulah lived a further six months, the hollow sound of the undertaker's feet eventually sounded on their stairway.

The bitterly cold winter of 1916 was followed by nothing but heavy rain the next year. Beulah's casket was manoeuvred through the small shop and then out into a downpour, where a single horse-drawn hearse stood waiting patiently. The funeral party moved slowly down the street towards the local chapel.

*

Some six weeks later, Sarah finally decided she could no longer withhold the truth concerning Jack's death, so, one evening, in their small sitting room, she endeavoured to break the news as gently as possible. Reaching across the table, she took Lilly's hand.

'I know,' she began, 'you were very impressed with the tall sergeant...' At which point, she paused, struggling for the right words. 'Anyway,' she managed. 'A few months ago, I came upon a newspaper that listed the men killed on the Somme and...'

But that was as far as she got as Lilly cried out in anguish, 'And my Jack was among them and you never told me!'

With that, she fled to the foot of the stairs in floods of tears.

Chapter 13

BUT, OF COURSE, Jack was not dead, for there were many men in the British Army with that name. However, he'd been lucky to survive to the end of the war with what the powers that be had in mind. After the heavy casualties suffered at Gallipoli, the Somme and Verdun, these powers were under severe pressure to come up with answers. As a result, early in December of 1916, the then British Prime Minister – Asquith – resigned, to be replaced by David Lloyd George. And it was this leader who, at a London conference on 10th January, agreed with the French General Robert Nivelle on what was to become known as the Nivelle offensive.

However, this is not a history lesson, but an account of one man's tribulation on his journey through the cataclysm that was the First World War. And it was not the planners who had to carry out these grandiose schemes, but the men on the ground like Jack – Jack, who, at this time, was still lying wounded in a grimy bombed-out farmhouse cellar. Perhaps this had one consolation, though, for there were always pretty nurses on hand with a cheerful word or the offer of help.

Early one morning, the sergeant awoke to find one such ministering angel sitting at the bottom of his cot.

'Hello, Jack,' she said, smiling gently. 'How are you feeling?'

He'd seen her previously flitting among the injured men, but this was their first direct encounter and, struggling up on one elbow, he winced as he felt his wounded shoulder.

'Well, I must admit,' he replied, with a lopsided grin, 'I've felt better, but thanks for asking.'

'I'm Alana and I just came to say how sorry I was to hear about Nurse Marian,' she explained. 'I got the impression you were quite close.'

The fact that his visitor was an attractive proposition had not escaped the sergeant, for, with her thick tresses of dark hair and full cupid-bow lips, she could well have been an older version of Lilly.

'What gave you the impression we were close?' he enquired cautiously. Her words had puzzled him.

She smiled. 'You only had to see the way she fussed over you when you were first brought in to know that something was going on. Anyway,' she announced, suddenly, while getting up, 'you have a visitor later this morning – a lieutenant colonel, no less.'

And with that and a swish of her skirts, she was gone.

Jack lay back and wondered why such a high-ranking person could possibly need to see him. He was soon to find out.

*

At 11am sharp, he was approached by an officer whose immaculate uniform gleamed with a multiplicity of brass work. The man held out his hand.

'Sergeant Miles?' he enquired briefly. As Jack nodded, he went on to explain the reason for his visit. 'I've come to congratulate you on the heroic way you got Major Van der Berg safely back to our lines.' He pointed to the sergeant's shoulder, adding, 'When you were wounded.'

Jack looked the officer straight in the eye.

'I had no option,' he murmured quietly. 'You see, he's my father.'

The officer looked mystified.

'But your name...?'

Jack shook his head.

'It's a long story.'

The colonel raised his eyebrows, before adding, 'There's a big push on the Aisne planned for April and your name has been put forward for a commission.' At the sergeant's lack of response, the officer shrugged. 'Anyway,' he said, preparing to leave, 'at least give it some thought.'

Jack did. However, he was all too familiar with the trench mantra, "Brass attracts bullets".

Chapter 14

THE SERGEANT'S WOUND took a long time to heal. It was also very painful and a nurse would often have to administer something to ease the discomfort. On one such occasion, it was the nurse who had sympathised with him over Marian. She never said much, but obviously admired what she saw. At times when Jack felt lonely or bored, he was tempted to take things a step further. However, there was Lilly. Then suddenly, it was all too late, as orders came through for an advance on Arras city.

On his final morning, he awoke to again find the same nurse sitting on his bed.

'Good morning, Jack,' she said quietly, with a hint of sadness. 'We say goodbye today.'

'You know,' he responded. 'But in a different time and a different place...'

She nodded while getting up. 'Yes, things might well have been very different.'

Overwhelmed by the emotion of the moment, the sergeant got to his feet and, towering over her, he slowly and deliberately took her in his arms. Then, with her figure pressing against him and her gentle

fragrance in the air, he bent to kiss her on the lips –
a kiss that provoked an almost aggressive response.
And that was the way they remained, despite a
certain whistling in the background.

However, even as they parted, a lieutenant poked
his head down the stairwell.

'The whole regiment's forming up at midday for
the advance on Arras city.'

The nurse looked up longingly at Jack. 'Will I
ever see you again?' she whispered.

However, the sergeant's dilemma was complete
and, committed to Lilly, he lied. 'If I can, I'll be back,
but,' he added, getting his equipment together, 'if
not...' He shrugged.

'Goodbye, Jack. I'll never forget you.'

Unable to meet her gaze, the sergeant headed for
the exit.

'If you want to contact me after the war,' she
called after him, 'I'll be based at the Bath hospital.'

It's doubtful he even heard her – or wanted to.
But that was then...

*

When Jack reached the parade ground, he was
staggered by what he saw, for there were literally
hundreds of lines of men arranged in regiments
and companies – ready, as it were, to face their fate
during the drive on Arras city. Men that represented
thousands of women back home, who would never
marry because so many would be killed.

In front of this vast assemblage stood a man that Jack took to be General Haig. Festooned with military honours, he was handing out final words of encouragement.

'Let's kick the Boche out of Europe once and for all,' he bellowed. Although, how near his foot would actually come to any of the enemy's backsides was probably an open question.

'Come,' said the lieutenant, 'let me introduce you to our replacement platoon.'

There were some fifty combatants that comprised the new group. Jack was horrified to see how fresh-faced many of them looked and doubted whether some were even seventeen. Their whole life in front of them was now in the balance.

The lieutenant was speaking again. 'You are already acquainted with Lance Corporal Simms. Well, he's been made up to corporal.'

Jack shook his hand before immediately having his attention drawn to a newcomer, who the lieutenant introduced as Corporal Gray. The sergeant looked carefully at the NCO and, if he was honest, he didn't like what he saw. The man avoided direct eye contact and exuded a certain shiftiness. Not the sort of individual the sergeant would have chosen in a tight corner.

Finally, instructions came through for the whole column to move – orders that rang out from the drill sergeants over and over again as each company took turns to right wheel. With such a body of men, the operation took time, but, finally, the unending river of khaki was on its way to Arras city. The question in Jack's mind was just how many of them would return.

That night, lying in a shallow trench not far from their objective, Jack let his mind wander over the intricacies of his life. It had seemed all so cosy to condemn his father's and aunt's immoral behaviour, but, after his experience with two women at the casualty station, these values didn't seem quite so clear-cut. Would he, in all honesty, remain faithful to Lilly if given the chance with the second nurse?

*

Early the following morning, however, he had other things to worry about – namely, his own safety and that of his men, for they were advancing towards the outskirts of the city itself, albeit in staggered blocks of four men. To a certain extent, they were protected by a new technique nicknamed the "creeping barrage". It was a very precise procedure and only allowed for the narrowest of errors, because it involved dropping shells right in front of their own men. It had the advantage, however, of keeping the enemy's head down until the last minute, which was essential as the area around Arras was infested with German mortar emplacements and machine-gun nests.

However, even with these precautions, a sudden burst of automatic fire wiped out a group advancing on Jack's right flank. It was a sight that sent the newly promoted Corporal Simms into a blind fury and, breaking formation, he grabbed two grenades from his battle pouch and lobbed them straight into the enemy's shallow dugout. The effect was electrifying, as earth and mangled bodies were thrown high into the air. It was a heroic act that deserved commendation, but, sadly, as the corporal moved back to rejoin his group, he stepped on a landmine – the force of which nearly blew Jack off his feet.

But if Jack had felt the blast, it was nothing compared to how it affected the brave NCO, for he was hurled up before falling back like a disjointed rag doll among the very enemy he had just destroyed.

However, the sergeant barely had time to witness his corporal's demise before a nearby mortar blast almost tore his leg from his body and he collapsed to the ground in agony, as the rapid loss of blood quickly brought on a state of semi-consciousness. He was only vaguely aware of the stretcher-bearers who came to his aid and carried him to the rear.

Well behind the lines yet still amid drifting gun smoke, the surgeons fought for hours to piece Jack's leg back together. Finally, through a mist of morphine and pain, the sergeant heard the doctor's verdict.

'Well, Sergeant,' explained the medic, with a round mirror still attached to his forehead. 'We managed to save your leg, but it will always be shorter than it was, so you'll probably have a permanent limp. I'm afraid the war's over for you, though. It's back to Blighty and a long period of recuperation at the Bath War Hospital.' He half smiled. 'I'll bet you're not sorry, because, from the look of your scars, you've more than done your bit.'

'Bath!' Jack strained to remember where he'd heard the name and, seeing the sergeant's perplexed expression, the medic hastened to explain.

'It's a rehabilitation centre for soldiers who have lost a limb or been badly maimed.'

At that point, the implication suddenly struck home. *Alana!*

Chapter 15

IF THE SERGEANT was absolutely honest, he'd be the first to admit feeling pissed off with lying in a ward full of injured and moaning men – many of whom had their limbs in plaster, strapped up at every conceivable angle.

One night, lying amid the moaning and the spewing, his thoughts turned to the absence of any correspondence from Lilly. Painful as it seemed, there appeared only one explanation. She'd found someone else. Finally, turning on his side as far as his injured leg would allow, he tried to sleep, determining to write to her the following day and find out the truth.

But Jack had never found it easy to chase after people and, after several attempts the next morning, he screwed up the last sheet of paper and tossed it to the foot of his bed. No sooner had it bounced to the floor than someone entered the ward who immediately grabbed his attention – and, incidentally, a lot of the other male patients as well.

There, striding between the beds, was no less than Alana – the nurse from the bombed-out farmhouse cellar. An expressive woman, she stopped at the foot of Jack's bed and struck a provocative pose.

'So, we meet again, Sergeant!'

Alana was, by any standards, a statuesque woman with all that implied, and Jack experienced a guilty thrill as he remembered the excitement of their one-off physical encounter. However, he was hardly in a position to repeat the exercise with his leg suspended at forty-five degrees to the ceiling.

Eyeing the debris on his bed, she caustically observed, 'And I suppose you've left that lot for me to clear up.' However, before he even had a chance to reply, she had plonked herself down and crossed her shapely legs. Then, without any warning, she let him have it very bluntly. 'You know,' she began, 'a lot of men find me very attractive.' This, in itself, sounded outrageous, but it was what followed that put Jack on the back foot – as far as his injuries would allow. 'But you see,' she continued, pointedly. 'The very few men that interest me don't seem to want to know.'

The sergeant knew full well to whom she was referring and he started to protest. 'Look, Alana. One passionate embrace doesn't constitute a relationship – although,' he hastened to add, 'as I said at the time, if things had been different...'

But this lady had the sensitivity of cast iron.

'What needs to be different?' she demanded. 'You obviously fancy me and I fancy you, so why the hell don't we just bugger off into the sunset?'

Talk about brash, the sergeant thought. *If I*

married a woman like that, it wouldn't be me that wore the trousers.

As Alana had been speaking, she'd picked over the screwed-up paper Jack had discarded earlier. '"My dearest Lilly,"' she read. '"I just wondered why I hadn't heard from you for so long." Oh!' she exclaimed. 'There's someone else. And this lot all looks a bit private.'

'Wait a minute,' pleaded Jack. 'Let me try and explain.'

But it was hopeless, for, with a brief wave and a goodbye, she was gone.

The sergeant lay back with a sigh of resignation, while a voice from his neighbour's bed expressing appreciation over his visitor did precious little to help. Jack stared at the whitewashed ceiling and his suspended leg for a long time. Attractive as she was, he knew life with someone like Alana would be far from easy. Physical attractions fade, but he wasn't so sure about a nagging tongue and he knew himself well enough to realise he was no yes-man.

Chapter 16

FINALLY, IN LATE October 1917, the sergeant found himself once more on his home soil. Disembarking at Portsmouth and looking smart in his demob suit, Jack made straight for his old lodgings in North Street, Portslade.

The war had brought little change to the narrow road. It was obviously still a very poverty-stricken area with small, pinched shopfronts that looked out desperately for any passing trade, while a good lick of paint on most of them would not go amiss. Then there were the handcarts being trundled forlornly up and down on their way to who knows where.

As the sergeant raised a hand to knock on the door of his old billet, he noticed one difference at the end of the street. The old Salvation Army HQ had been converted into what, in those days, was referred to as The Prince's Imperial Picture Palace. It seemed perverse that something originally dedicated to the glory of God had become a centre for secular entertainment.

As these thoughts flashed through his mind,

the door suddenly swung back to reveal his old, but startled, landlord.

'Why, Sergeant Jack!' cried the householder. 'We all thought you were dead.'

'Well, I've had several close calls, I must admit,' stressed the ex-soldier. Then, after being invited into the familiar little hallway, he asked, 'What made you think I was a goner?'

In such a confined space, Jack seemed to tower over his host – an elderly man in his early seventies, who everyone referred to as Ben.

'Oh,' he replied, nodding towards the street. 'I happened to bump into the cobbler's wife. You know, the lady from the shoe shop. Apparently, she'd read about it in some newspaper.'

'So that's why she never wrote,' muttered the sergeant as he made for the door. 'She thought I'd been killed.'

'If you mean Lilly,' protested Ben. 'You can't just go in there bald-faced and say, "Hey, guess what? I'm alive." Can you imagine what her old man's reaction would be? He's a miserable old sod at the best of times. No, I think it would be far better if I dropped in a quiet note later this evening.' Sadly, this quiet note would never materialise. Age, it seemed, had eroded Ben's memory. 'Look,' he added. 'Why don't you make yourself at home in the snug while I rustle up a pot of tea? Then we can bring each other up to date. I can tell you, it's been a sad few years around these parts.'

When Jack stepped into what Ben had referred to

as the snug, it was as though three years just melted away. Could it really be possible, he wondered, that so much time had passed since he was last there? The relatively small room was fronted by a bay window that looked directly out onto the street. It was a place that spoke of dedication on the one hand and a lack of money on the other, for Ben's wife had worked tirelessly on a limited budget to create a comfortable retreat for soldiers far from home. Dominated by a worn but lovingly patched-up three-piece suite, there was an almost timeless air about the space – a quality interrupted by a small marble clock on the mantlepiece that remorselessly ticked away the passing years.

For several moments, Jack just stood in the doorway as the memories came flooding back – memories of his time billeted there along with two other infantrymen. Days when the room had rocked with laughter and when world's problems had been solved with light banter. Now, all that was gone and only a heavy silence prevailed.

Wandering across the threadbare carpet, he paused to gaze down at one of the fireside armchairs. Little Joe's armchair. Like Jack's corporal, Joe had been a diminutive guardsman from the valleys. And also like the corporal, he had possessed a laugh capable of slicing through steel. Where was he now?

Moving to the window, he hooked a finger over the top of the faded net curtain and peered along the street, where it was just possible to see the little shoe shop situated on the far corner. However, as he was about to turn away, he noticed a young boy immediately opposite busily bowling a wooden hoop along the pavement – a common sight in 1917. Disaster then struck as the youngster suddenly lost control of his toy and it ended up under the hooves of a passing horse and cart.

The hoop was smashed to matchwood while the driver was hard put to control his terrified animal. Jack could only watch as the cart's steel-rimmed wheels mounted the kerb and crashed into an adjoining shopfront. The result was pandemonium, with curiosity-seekers converging from every direction. Worse, the force of the impact had been so great that the driver was hurled onto the pavement where he lay in an inert heap. What the sergeant had no means of knowing was that he had just witnessed the precursor of far worse events to come.

'Tea up, Jack!' came Ben's voice as he entered the room laden with a tray of rattling cups.

'You should see that lot out there,' responded the old soldier, releasing the net curtain.

Meanwhile, the horse had kicked over the traces and was now galloping off down the street, dragging one of the broken shafts along the kerb.

'Chaos!' exclaimed Ben as he joined Jack at the window. 'Absolute chaos. By the look of it, there are enough busybodies out there to sort it out.'

Then, turning from the circus outside, Jack asked if Ben knew what had become of the two Welsh guardsmen who had stayed there towards the end of 1914.

'Both dead,' was the blunt reply. Ben heaved a sigh as he indicated for Jack to take a seat in one of the fireside armchairs. Little Joe's chair. 'Very sad,' he continued as he poured his guest a cup of tea. 'Both died on the Somme last year. About the same time that I lost my wife.'

'Jennifer's gone?' exclaimed Jack. 'I can't believe it. I mean, she was quite a bit younger than you, I thought. What...'

'TB,' murmured Ben bitterly, taking a seat opposite. 'It's the bloody scourge of our time. It was what took your Lilly's sister, Beulah. I told you, it's been a bad few years.'

On hearing this, Jack shook his head. 'I knew she had an older sister, though I never actually saw her. Poor Lilly. How awful.'

For several moments, Ben stared vacantly into a distance that only he could see, then said, 'She was a lovely girl. And beautiful... you wouldn't believe it. She gradually seemed to waste away. And that cough...'

For a while, the two men sat in a subdued silence as the end of the day approached and the light gradually began to fade.

Finally, Jack spoke, 'I was wondering, Ben, if perhaps you could put me up for a few days.'

At this, the old boy's face immediately brightened. 'Jack,' he responded. 'I'd be only too delighted. It gets very lonely here without my wife and you can have the room you shared with Little Joe and Harold.'

*

The following day, sunlight was streaking the eastern sky as Jack made his way downstairs and headed for the kitchen, from which emanated a very appetising smell. Ben was already there, bent over the stove – although, hearing his guest's approach, he looked up with a smile.

'Bacon and egg, Jack?'

The sergeant sat down at the kitchen table.

'Well!' he exclaimed. 'That would certainly be very welcome after the diet on the Western Front. Over there, it was bully beef. Take it or leave it. And,' he stressed, 'a lot of the lads suffered from scurvy as a result.' He paused to glance round the kitchen. It was small and old, and lighting was dependent on a single gas mantle. Perhaps the little room's only redeeming feature was a tiny south-facing window, which afforded distant views of the Channel. Getting up for a moment, Jack gazed out at the sea with its foam-topped rollers, as they came crashing in over the shingle before drawing back to repeat the process again and again.

'There we are!' exclaimed Ben, as he shovelled generous portions onto Jack's plate. 'Let's see you get through that lot.'

The sergeant, who had not eaten since lunchtime the previous day, quickly made inroads.

'Thanks, Ben. That was very welcome. I wondered if you happen to know where I could buy some flowers for Lilly.'

'Ah,' replied the landlord, sitting down to his own breakfast. 'That I can help you with.' Carving a slice of bacon, he added, 'Go down to the corner by the shoe shop and turn left into the high street. There's a new flower shop right opposite Mrs Trill's tea shop. Mind you,' he added between mouthfuls, 'they must only make any money from weddings and funerals. Who in these parts can afford the luxury of flowers? They can barely afford to eat. In fact, I believe that poor girl, Beulah, only succumbed to TB through a lack of nourishment. Yet,' he shrugged, 'her old man's always down the boozer. It doesn't make sense.'

Jack drew a deep breath as he prepared to leave, but unwittingly made a fatal error by omitting to ask Ben if he'd dropped in the promised note concerning his survival.

Chapter 17

CONSIDERING THE TIME of year, the day proved to be an exceptionally sunny one as the sergeant stepped into the street. However, seeing the boarded-up shopfront was a sharp reminder of the previous day's accident. Turning to the right, Jack made his way briskly past the corner shoe shop and into the high street where, sure enough, just across the road, there was a flower shop – the frontage of which was festooned with a sea of brightly coloured blossoms.

Roses, thought Jack. *Lots of cheerful roses.*

Entering the shop to the tinkle of its bell, he found himself faced with a slim, middle-aged man.

'Yes? Is there something I can do for you?' the man enquired as he moved forward.

Jack asked to be shown some roses and, after much dithering and twittering, a quite beautiful array of blooms had been assembled. Then, with a deft movement, the proprietor held out his hand for the requisite seven shillings and sixpence. Handing over a ten-shilling note, Jack took the bouquet and told the assistant to keep the change.

Back in the high street, Jack was about to

experience the greatest tragedy of his life, for coming out of North Street was Lilly – the girl he planned to marry. The girl who believed him to be dead.

Catching sight of the sergeant, she screamed out loud, 'Jack! Is that really you? Oh, Jack.'

In her emotionally charged state, she made to cross the road to take him in her arms. However, mindlessly stepping off the kerb in her haste, she failed to notice an approaching horse-drawn bus and fell headfirst under the leading animal's hooves. Stumbling over something under its feet, the fear-ridden animal kicked and stamped to get itself free. For Lilly, it was the end. An appalling and agonising death. Jack could only watch helplessly as the enormity of the horror unfolded before his eyes.

Flinging the roses to the ground, he raced across the road. Powerfully built as he was, he shouldered the horse to one side, but, from his former wartime experience, one glance was sufficient to tell him he was too late. Oh, far too late.

'Careful of the 'orse.'

The driver had come down from the front of the bus and, although shocked by the accident, he still had a responsibility for the two animals. However, the sergeant, lost in the red mists of hell, lashed out at the man with such force that he was lifted off his feet and sent crashing back into the gathering crowd of onlookers. Then, sinking down on his knees in the middle of the road, Jack gathered up his precious, broken Lilly, while sobbing, 'No. No.'

With her bleeding head held against his chest, he

looked up questioningly at the sky, but the heavens, as the expression goes, were as brass. There was no help to be had from that direction. Ironically, the whole tragedy had taken place almost right outside Mrs Trill's seedy tea shop where he and Lilly had first enjoyed a lunchtime date together.

On the pavement outside the flower shop, the scattered roses seemed to cry out a sad lament. Meant to be a celebration of their reunion, they had become Lilly's wreath. Gently, Jack gathered them up before placing them reverently at her side. Finally, and inevitably, the time came to leave her – to leave her to those who dealt with such things. Kissing her gently, he got up and pushed his way through the crowd of those who seemed to feast on the misfortune of others. Not that he noticed, but even Mrs Trill was busy getting her two penn'orth through the grimy window of her tea shop.

*

By the time Jack had retraced his steps to the door of his old lodgings, he was in a state of mental collapse.

'What on earth...' gasped Ben as he answered the sergeant's frantic knocking.

Standing there was a man with his shirt smothered in blood – a man, in fact, for whom life had lost its meaning.

'Lilly's dead,' Jack just about managed as he stumbled up the front step and into the hallway.

'Dead!' exclaimed the old landlord. 'How can

she be? I saw her out and about only the day before yesterday.'

The ex-sergeant was shaking from head to foot as Ben took him by the arm and led him into the snug, where he collapsed into Little Joe's chair.

'Ben,' Jack cried, looking up. 'She saw me unexpectedly in the high street and stepped straight out under a bus. I watched her, Ben.' He sobbed with tears rolling down his face. 'I watched as those two bloody animals trampled her to pieces and there was nothing I could do. Nothing!'

At this, the old man felt a sudden pang of guilt as he remembered the note he had promised and failed to drop in. He realised the terrible shock it must have been for poor Lilly to see the sergeant alive and well.

'Listen, Jack, I'll just nip to the kitchen and get you some brandy.' Glad to get away for a moment, he left the sergeant alone with his grief, before returning with a bottle.

Dejected beyond speech, Jack grabbed the brandy bottle and swallowed its contents like lemonade.

'Careful,' Ben warned. 'That's powerful stuff.'

'Look,' replied Jack, handing over a five-pound note. 'Do me a favour and get another couple of bottles.'

Taking the hint, Ben left the room again.

Sitting in Little Joe's chair gave Jack a view of the bright blue sky, which was just visible above the rooftops opposite – a bright day. How ironic!

Burying his face in his hands, Jack let his mind wander back over the events that had led him to this agonising point in time – events, it seemed, that had been almost unendingly tragic and he was barely twenty-five years old. The loss of his home and mother in Wellborn Street; the death of his friend, Marian, by a bullet that was almost certainly meant for him; the loss of his one true friend, Michael. Not to mention nearly being parted from his right leg in a mortar blast. And now this final catastrophe that had robbed him of any future happiness as a married man.

When Ben returned, he deemed it wiser to just put the two bottles by Jack's chair and quietly leave the room.

Gradually, the sky began to dim with the approach of night. The sergeant didn't move except to reach for the brandy. Finally, and perhaps mercifully, he sank into a deep and intoxicated slumber.

*

Jack didn't attend Lilly's funeral. It was something he just couldn't face, preferring instead to remain in an alcoholic haze at his lodgings. In fact, for the next six months, he barely moved from Little Joe's chair and it came to a point when Ben began to become extremely worried over Jack's mental health. Finally, after finding him one morning at around 11am still in a drunken stupor, Ben gave voice to his concerns. However, Jack didn't take kindly to being shaken out of his alcohol-fuelled oblivion and said so in no uncertain and slurred terms.

'Look, I pay you good rent. Bugger off and leave me alone.'

And so, his alcoholic state continued, until one night he had a very strange experience, and for years afterwards he could never quite determine whether it had been a dream or some weird kind of reality. He suddenly found himself back at The Toby Jug, where everything appeared incredibly clear and sharp. Sitting in his old seat, he ran his fingers along the edge of the table he'd always shared with Michael and it all felt oh so familiar.

Looking up, he caught the eye of the barmaid, who waved in recognition. And there, unbelievably, was Michael, crossing the floor and carrying two drinks. However, upon reaching the table, his old friend didn't say a word, but simply passed over one of the froth-topped tankards.

Sitting down, Michael took a draught of his drink. 'You're letting me down,' he finally said.

Jack was puzzled. 'Letting you down? How? And in what way?'

'During the war,' continued his old friend, 'you promised me faithfully to live life for the both of us.'

Suddenly stricken with remorse, Jack looked down for a moment before reaching out to clasp his friend's hand, only to recoil for it had no substance. Glancing up, Jack could see no sign of his visitor – only an empty chair and his untouched glass of beer, which was still on the table.

At that moment, Jack awoke with a start to find himself back in Little Joe's armchair. However, his hitherto befuddled mind had been replaced by some very focused thinking. Live a life for two, Michael had said. And that was just what he intended to do – to keep his solemn promise to the sad bundle he had laid to rest in a distant war grave.

*

With nothing left to keep him in the Portslade area, Jack determined to return to his aunt in Croydon. Before he left, he made one last call at the little corner shoe shop. As the doorbell tinkled at his entry, Lilly's younger sister, Daisy, glanced up. The effect on the sergeant was devastating, because, for a split second, he thought he was looking at Lilly.

'Why, Sergeant!' she exclaimed. 'To what do we owe this pleasure?'

'I just called in,' Jack began, hesitantly, 'to say how sorry I am over the loss of your sister. I'm so, so sorry.' He momentarily glanced down at the floor as if ashamed, before admitting, 'I'm afraid I just couldn't bring myself to attend the funeral.'

'Jack,' she replied quietly, 'I do understand.' Then she added earnestly, 'You know, Lilly did love you. She really did.'

Overcome with emotion, the ex-soldier felt the tears gather in his eyes. Turning away, he limped towards the door where he turned and waved.

'Take care of yourself, Daisy,' he whispered. 'Take really great care of yourself.'

With that, he stepped back into the street and

quietly closed the door. However, this was not just the closing of any door, but the symbolic end of a dream. Turning his steps towards the railway station, Jack resolutely set out to begin a new life – two new lives, in fact.

*

When Eva opened the front door and saw her nephew, her joy knew no bounds and she unreservedly flung her arms around his neck.

'Why, Jack! How lovely to see you. Come on in, but what's happened to your leg?' she asked, noticing his pronounced limp. 'Never mind that. Come through to the lounge.' Then, over a strong cup of black coffee, Jack recounted his recent sad experiences.

'Oh, Jack. I'm so sorry,' she responded. 'How awful for you. What will you do now?'

'Well,' he replied, leaning forward in his armchair, 'I had hoped to stay with you for a few days, but, tell me, is Brownlow's still in the high street?'

'You're welcome to stay as long as you like,' Eva assured him. 'As regards the butcher, I think he's on the point of retirement.'

*

The upshot of this prompted the sergeant to buy out the aging butcher and assume his role. However, if Jack was to keep his promise to Michael, he knew he had to find a wife and have a family, for he was sure that's what his friend would have done. Deep down, he was certain he knew just the girl – someone feisty, who was not afraid to speak their mind, and with a figure... It wouldn't be easy with such a sassy woman, but Jack nevertheless determined to contact Alana. If ever there was enough woman for two men, she was the one – although he had no illusions about his own prowess in that department.

Therefore, three weeks later saw the sergeant leaning up against the doorpost of one of the wards at the injured soldiers' rehabilitation centre in Bath. When Alana finally appeared, he had to admit she was something else. However, there was always the tongue that went with it.

'Oh! Down from the beanstalk again, are we?' she exclaimed, upon catching sight of Jack. 'What have you brought down this time? Two golden eggs or the hen?'

It has to be wondered what the poor man could have said in the face of such sarcasm. However, Jack was no ordinary man and, prising himself away from the door jam, he towered over her with his full six feet three inches.

'Has anyone ever told you that you can be rude? Bloody rude!'

Taken aback, the nurse fell silent before observing in a subdued voice, 'You're about the only man I've ever really fancied and, yes, I get rude knowing you belong to someone else.'

At this, Jack took her by the elbow and steered

her away from the ward. 'Hey! Where are you taking me?' she protested. 'I'm on duty.'

'To hell with on duty,' insisted Jack. 'You and I have got to talk.'

Finally, with both seated in the hospital restaurant and with coffees in front of them, the sergeant leaned across the table and pressed a small square box into her hand.

'I didn't bring any golden eggs, as you put it. I brought you this instead. And before you open it, I must tell you it was bought especially for you and no one else.'

Unable to believe what was happening, Alana slowly lifted the lid, which allowed a diamond-encrusted gold engagement ring to flash and sparkle its brilliance. As she went to lift it from its box, the sergeant reached over and deftly slipped it on the third finger of her left hand.

'Will you wear it for me?' he said simply.

And there, in the mundane surroundings of the refectory, she nodded, speechless with joy.

After some time, however, the words came. 'Is this,' she began breathlessly, 'some kind of proposal? I mean, I thought there was someone else.'

Jack knew he had to choose his next words with care. 'There was someone else,' he began cautiously, 'but you must understand that was only because I met her first.'

For a long time, Alana gazed at the back of her hand with its glittering ring. Then, as a more sober sense of reality set in, she looked Jack straight in the eye.

'So, what has changed to make things different now?'

Jack looked down at his untouched coffee, again knowing that he had to be very careful with what he said.

'The lady I intended to marry got killed in a tragic road accident. To make matters worse, I witnessed the whole thing – but,' he emphasised, 'that was then and I've moved on. And if you'd accept that ring, I'd be honoured to have you as my wife.'

'Oh, Jack,' she gasped, rushing round the table and hugging him by the neck. 'Nothing could make me happier.' She laughingly added, 'I, Alana, do hereby promise to take you, Jack, and your beanstalk, to be my lawful wedded husband.'

Nearby ears had already been flapping at right angles and when Jack got to his feet and took her in his arms, a number of heads began to turn.

Briefly pulling away, Jack murmured, 'I believe we could be very happy – although you do sometimes have a very straight way of talking.'

'You mean,' she said bluntly, 'that I have a sharp tongue! I know it's true, but I promise you faithfully, I will never, ever use it on you. I value you far too much.'

In due course, Jack and Alana became husband and wife. True to her word, she was always careful to keep her vow.

*

Although the sergeant kept the sign "Brownlow & Son" over the butcher's shop, it soon became popularly known as Jack and Alana's, for the new Mrs Miles often helped out with the customers. Her attractiveness was never lost on the male patrons, but she only ever had eyes for her strapping husband.

The sergeant always remembered his promise to Michael and did his best to enjoy life, with the result that he and his wife were frequent visitors to Croydon's Saturday night dance.

However, the years inevitably rolled by and, suddenly it seemed, they found themselves in the middle of the twenties – or "the roaring twenties" as they came to be known. The Charleston was all the rage and no one was better at the dance than Alana. With her short frilly skirt and miles of endless necklaces, together with tightly plaited hair, she became a phenomenon on the dance floor.

Originating from Charleston in South Carolina, America, the dance seemed to represent a resurgence of human energy after the appalling losses of the First World War. Despite his gammy leg, Jack was only too thankful to have survived to be part of it.

*

Time inexorably marched on and, by their early fifties, he and Alana were the proud parents of two beautiful teenage daughters and a twenty-year-old son.

When he had bought the butcher's shop, Jack

had acquired a thriving business – although perhaps it was the social aspect of the trade that he enjoyed rather than its actual commercial success. With the shop and a happy marriage to Alana, the dark shadows that had stalked his earlier years began to fade – until early one morning.

He was busy with the bacon slicer when the tinkling of the shop doorbell caused him to look up. He saw a very old and feeble woman shuffling her way across the floor towards the counter. Having reached her objective, she looked up at him through pebble-thick glasses.

'Just three slices of back rasher, please, Mr Brownlow,' she asked in a quavery voice.

Her sight was obviously very poor – a weakness of age reflected by her dependency on two walking sticks.

'I'm sorry,' responded the butcher, 'but I'm not Mr Brownlow. He retired years ago.'

As he spoke, he recognised something familiar about the old lady and suddenly realised he was looking at an aging Mrs Marshall. A vision of her daughter, Marian, virtually dying in his arms, flooded back into his mind as though it had been yesterday. Suddenly, he was back at the bottom of the stairwell in the bombed-out and shattered ruins of the field hospital close to the Western Front, while the last words of her gentle voice rang in his ears.

'Jack. I could have so loved you.'

He felt the tears prick at the corners of his eyes and threaten to run down his cheeks, as he faced the dilemma of declaring his true identity and the emotional overtures that were bound to follow. However, as it happened, the decision was made for him as the old lady peered up at his tall frame.

'I know you,' she quavered. 'You're Jack, aren't you?'

'Yes, ma'am,' he admitted. 'That's just who I am.'

She paused to look up at him warmly. 'I remember how happy you made my daughter at the town hall dance all those years ago. She looked forward to it so much and talked about nothing else for weeks afterwards.'

At that point, though, it seemed the effort of standing overtook her and she sank gracefully down onto the chair Jack had so thoughtfully provided for his older clients.

After a long pause, she added, 'I'm so grateful to you for making her happy that evening.' She paused again before continuing, 'I think you know she had hoped you might call on her again, but...' Her voice trailed off with a hint of sadness.

'I nearly did,' Jack heard himself murmur, giving a guilty shrug. 'Your daughter was a very sweet girl, but, you see,' he explained, 'I'd had a number of bitter experiences and it had made me cautious.'

For a long time, the old girl just sat there slumped in the chair, her hands resting on one of her walking sticks. Finally, however, with her eyes dimmed by sadness, she gazed at Jack.

'She's dead, you know. She volunteered to help nurse the war's injured and got killed trying to help others. She's buried somewhere out in France and I can't even visit her grave.' The old girl paused again. 'Such a pity and she would have made someone such a lovely wife.'

Jack knew all this, of course, only too well, but wisely decided not to elaborate on the fact too much. Instead, in order to offer a grain of comfort, he explained how she had died in his arms, fully aware of who he was.

Finally, struggling to her feet, Mrs Marshall repeated her request for the three rashers of bacon, which Jack promptly cut from a joint on the slicing machine before folding them in a sheet of greaseproof paper and handing them to his aging customer.

'How much will that be?' she enquired, in a slightly broken voice.

Jack shook his head. 'No charge.'

As he watched her hobble to the door, he heard a voice enquiring, 'And who was it that would have made such a lovely wife, may I ask?'

Alana, having cleared the breakfast things away, had come to help out in the shop. She'd arrived just in time to hear the last of the conversation with Mrs Marshall.

At first, Jack didn't reply, but leaned his elbows on the chopping block while rubbing his hands over his face as if to wipe away the troubling thoughts. When he finally spoke, it was in hushed tones, 'You remember the field hospital near the Somme and how that young nurse was killed by a German sniper?'

'Yes,' murmured his wife. 'I seem to think she was a bit sweet on you.'

'Well, that may be,' he responded in the same subdued voice, while staring down at the chopping board, 'but that lady,' he added, nodding towards the door, 'was her mother. And she's heartbroken by the death of her daughter. As far as I know, she lives all alone.'

Silence reigned in the butcher's shop for several moments before Alana spoke again. 'Very sad,' she agreed, quietly. 'The war's got a lot to answer for. I'm just thankful you were lucky enough to survive. You say she lives alone?' his wife queried. 'But what about her husband?'

Jack let his gaze wander over to the row of carcasses opposite as they dripped blood onto the sawdust floor.

'As far as I know,' he began, 'he deserted her for another woman shortly after they first got married.' *Life can be very cruel*, thought Jack. *Very cruel. If anyone ought to know, it's me.*

Standing there with both hands resting on the counter, he found the spectacle of Mrs Marshall's distress unexpectedly triggering thoughts of his own lost mother. He'd been barely six when she'd left him with her half-sister, Eva. He remembered so clearly how she'd taken him in her arms and assured him of her love. From that day onwards, though, he had never seen her again. Now in his mid-fifties, he wondered if she was even still alive. The bitterness of it all had hitherto caused him to repress all thoughts of her.

'Are you alright, Jack?' enquired Alana, seeing his strained expression.

'Yes, yes, I'm fine!' he exclaimed as he straightened up. 'I just got caught out by some unpleasant memories. They'll pass.'

His wife moved across the shop and put her arms around him in a gesture of comfort.

'Is it anything you'd like to share?' she whispered tenderly.

As he held her close, he murmured, 'You know, you've never been anything but kind and loving.'

'You mean,' she said, smiling up at him, 'despite the possible threat of my tongue.'

And there, in the middle of the shop, oblivious to everything else, they remained in a loving embrace.

Mrs Marshall had left the door open, so there was no warning bell when the next customer came in until reality came crashing down in the form of a cough and a polite enquiry.

'Excuse me, but is it possible to be served...?'

*

The decades continued to roll by in a seemingly unstoppable flow. Alana had always been a robust and strong woman, but with the onset of old age, her health began to fail and she became increasingly dependent on a walking frame. One night, while in bed, and with the room bathed in soft moonlight, she turned to face her husband.

'Jack,' she began gently, 'we've been together

a long time. Tell me truthfully, have I managed to make you happy? I know I was your second choice.'

The old sergeant took her in his arms. 'Darling,' he assured her. 'You couldn't possibly have made me any happier.' Drawing her closer, he added, 'And I must have told you a hundred times you were never my second choice.'

Alana looked up at him adoringly, yet with a certain wistful sadness.

'We have been happy, haven't we?' Then, with a mischievous twinkle in her eye, she continued, 'And I've never exposed you to my sharp tongue, have I?'

Silence reigned for several moments before she exclaimed, in an almost inaudible voice, 'But one day soon, we'll have to part, won't we?'

All Jack could do was nod dumbly. 'One day.'

'Oh, Jack,' she cried, suddenly, clutching at his arm. 'I'm so afraid.'

'Of what? There's nothing to fear. You're always safe with me,' he assured her.

With pleading in her eyes, she murmured, 'I'm frightened of leaving you and the children.' She then uttered the eternal uncertainty of the human race, 'You see, if I'm honest, I'm afraid of dying.' Looking him in the eyes, she added, 'Aren't you afraid?'

In an attempt to reassure her, the old soldier described his vision of the dead army nurse, Marian, and how he'd seen her with her rejuvenated mother in a beautiful orchard. He went on to describe the exquisite peace. 'It might only have been a dream...' he went on.

But by then, Alana had fallen into a deep and contented sleep.

Their bedroom windows were immediately above the butcher's shop and faced east, which gave a clear view of the new dawn as it sent streaks of light flooding across the sky, while the mellow moon had long since surrendered to the new day.

But it was at daybreak that Jack was to awake and find himself alone once more.

The plague that had robbed him of his mother at an early age and stolen his chances with Marian and Lilly had struck again. Now his wife lay beside him, stiff and cold in death. In life, Alana, had been such a vibrant and lively person, someone who could dance with exuberance without tiring, and it made him wonder what life was all about – some perverted accident or some unknown force that took delight in the miseries.

Epilogue

HAVING READ AND, I hope, enjoyed the story of Sergeant Jack, I thought the reader might like to know his character is based upon the experience of a real person.

Jack's mother was indeed a cook at Hereford Castle where his father had been a visiting baker. Jack was born into the world technically a cockney. He left school at the early age of eleven and served as an apprentice in the butchery trade, later training as a slaughterman. His promise was such that the local authority offered him the post of meat inspector for the area – a position he felt unable to take up due to his lack of education.

But, about that time, he was called up to serve as an army sergeant in the First World War – a war which sadly saw the death of his friend Sergeant Michael and Jack undertook his burial. Michael was a man whose name is recorded to this day on the Arlington War Memorial

Age shall not weary them, nor the years condemn.
Nice words that conceal an absolute tragedy.

Jack's ability as a sergeant came to the attention of the military hierarchy who offered him a commission in the field, but again it was an offer he refused due to his lack of education.

Back on the home front, after being severely wounded in the battle of Arras city, Jack settled down to court Violet, the daughter of a rather brutish shoe repairman – a man with whom he nearly came to blows on a number of occasions. Nevertheless, after the inordinate length of some twenty years, he finally got her to the altar.

Jack was born in the October of 1888 and died in the June of 1975. He was a man I was proud to have known.

How am I familiar with these facts?

You see, Sergeant Jack happened to be my father.